C000139884

the

ITERATION

Book # 1 of the XREAL Series

by

Will Lorimer

First Edition, published in 2022 by Inkistan.com.

Copyright © Will Lorimer

This book is copyright under the Berne
Convention.
No reproduction without permission.
® and © Inkistan.com. All rights reserved.

The right of Will Lorimer to be identified as the
author of this work has been
asserted in accordance with sections 77 and 78 of
the Copyright, Design and Patents Act, 1988.

Any similarity to persons living, dead or unborn,
is solely in the mind of the beholder, and any
correspondence to places, locales or events,
whether present, past or future, is entirely
coincidental.

Paperback: ISBN 978-1-7398776-7-5

Cover design, Will Lorimer

For Brodie and Rhea

SMOG FORECAST for The City and the wider Bay Area, today, Friday 6th August.

Smog cover is expected to be moderate, with an upper limit of 1200ft inland with some thinning around the coast from mid-morning, due to the S.E wind, but considerably thickening further out to sea, with an upper limit of 8,000ft at the Sound.

Maximum visibility (DBH), at the surface of 10ft to 15ft, is expected at noon.

Analysis of the particulate content, at 5am local time, taken at the City Eye monitoring station (see graphs) was Sulphurics 7.2 4 Organics,12.2, Calcium 24.3 with a virus load of 175 PM2.

For the 15th consecutive day, the Health Hazard Warning remains at Code Red.

Yesterday, a further 17 deaths attributed to smog-related conditions were recorded in the City and Bay area, bringing the total since the start of the Emergency to 21006.

When Jake Cousins pushed up the roof hatch and clambered out onto the Pierspoint Building roof, where dust lay thick, it was a rare blue-sky day. So much for the forecast, he thought, and how different from the view out of his workroom window earlier that morning, which had been that of a bottom feeder in a scummy fish pond, rather than from an apartment he had bought for the views.

Trying not to scuff up the toxic dust, Jake crept out from concealment. He moved between the rusty supports of the big old water tank that supplied the apartments below, ducking down behind the low parapet wall to look out over the rumpled folds of the blanketing smog, which spread in all directions and was only punctured here and there by the tops of tall buildings. They floated on the mirk, like the distant outposts of a drowned empire, glittering in sharp sunlight.

Everything else in the City was banished from sight, but not from mind. The streets below had been deserted since the Emergency had been declared three years before, except for the frenetic traffic of autonomous units serving the needs of the shut-in population. All day, every day, pac-bots and the ubiquitous whizzes dodged the plodding sweeps, without which the dust would be deep on the sidewalks instead of heaped in regular piles for collection by the vac-bots, which trailed behind like lost dogs. Down in the harbor, the wharves were empty too. No cruise ships berthed to disgorge flood-tides of day trippers into crowded plazas beyond the docks, who'd gawp up at the vacant plinths of statues that, less than a century after they were erected, had been removed because the past they commemorated was deemed shameful, before passing on to finger the tourist trinkets at stalls in the street markets, queuing for a ride on the big wheel, buying tickets to the many museums and art galleries, or, if feeling adventurous, taking the funicular to the terminal on Pierspoint Hill and looking down on the City from the battlements of McReadie's Fort, which was fake. And when they finally got back to the harbor, exhausted from so much sightseeing, they would not now rest weary feet and watch the street buskers from pavement cafes, bars and restaurants, around crowded plazas and lining the side streets, before the cruise ship's hooter sounded and it was time to do the same in another destination.

All gone, together with workers of the ghost offices in the new port development, its crowning glory the five-year-old shopping mall modelled on St. Peters of Rome, which had prompted a papal bull from the Vatican, citing it as a prime example of the satanic architecture of the corporate sector. The gross chrome and steel ribbing of its soaring dome was double the height of the original and stained with the stigmata of sea birds roosting on the cupula. They looked down from their perches on the flat roof of the grey metal Shoebox, now the headquarters of the City Eye, in which (even had it not been for the smog) neither windows nor entrance could be discerned.

Further round the Bay, where the smog was patchy, another signature building also marked the end of an era. A huge sports stadium, built for the cancelled Olympics Games, its unique half-marathon spiral running track looping the stands, a bridge to nowhere ending in a pointing long finger levelled at the blackened wastes on the wrong side of the 12 lane e-way and the vast sprawling Firebrick Estate where jet planes had been assembled in giant sheds before the flight paths over Siberia were shut down. Now, autonomous cranes, drilling rigs, huge excavators, humpers and scurries and a swarm of smaller bots were clearing the site next to the giant sheds of FauxReel International– the media wing of FakeReal(tm) where immersive verities continued to be made despite the Emergency that had shut down other industries.

Out beyond the City limits, way around the Bay, camps of the homeless mushroomed in the new swamplands formed when the coastal defenses were breached in the regular storms that now swept the coast.

All that crap gone, all those confined lives, all that misery blotted out by the Siberian smog which had shut down the City and shut in the citizens when the Emergency was declared three years before. Since then, the long smog had spread, of course, and now blanketed the northern hemisphere in a toxic stew of trace exotic minerals and unknown permafrost viruses released by burning Siberian peat, any of which the scientists declared could be highly transmissible and prove deadly.

Mostly, however, the smog was heavy with calcium from the bones of animals that had burrowed, roamed, wriggled, or flown over the tundra, mammoths to tiny shrews, hunter gatherers to the great leather-winged archaeopteryx dinosaurs, precursors of birds. Unaccounted billions of creatures, great and small, petrified in the peat over millions of years and turned to The Ash Of The Dead by the slow permafrost burn and associated methane blowholes which ejaculated unpredictably up to 30,000 feet and had brought down passenger planes.

The burn smoldered in a broad front around the Arctic Circle, from Kamkatcha to the fjords of Norway. The fires in Canada were out of control too, but at least there the jet stream carried the smoke over the Atlantic to Europe, where conditions were as bad or worse - and they were getting it from both east and west, if blogs on the FakeReal were to be believed.

But he was lucky, Jake reminded himself, glancing down at the watch that had belonged to his grandfather, the sweep of the second hand informing him he had precisely 59 seconds of freedom left before the City Eye's thermal imaging satellite pinpointed his position. Yes, Fortune had smiled on him like a favored son. If he hadn't sold his share of the architectural design company before it floated on the market, he'd have lost the lot like his former partners in the Crash of '27. Then, after the slump had bottomed out when he was just 28, he'd bought in at the old Pierspoint, if only by virtue of the craggy bluff it commanded and was named after. It was still the highest building in the City and, in his opinion, the most futuristic, with its truncated shape and copper sheathing gone green with age, resembling the cut off prow of a great ocean-going ship of a bygone age. The advanced techniques employed in its construction and the legends attached to the sounds the sub-structure generated in high winds had unfairly earned the Pierspoint an evil reputation in the City and a high occupancy turnover, depressing the once-astronomical prices of the apartments.

However, for Jake, the final deciding factor, persuading him to stake everything he had in his ultimately successful bid, had come when perusing the original plans of the building in the City Archives. With his architect's nous, he saw what no one else had, and the opportunity presented by the disused ventilation shaft to the roof, which had been covered up when the apartment was converted from some storage rooms some years before.

Now, Jake sighed, his attention drawn to the distant cowls of the three towers bobbing like drunken ducks on a sea of Siberian snot from over the horizon, where the smog was thickest, way out in the Sound. Each tower 10,000 feet high. They had to be, that was how they were sold. Numbers were very significant to the Man, who, after all, had more zeros banked than the nearest 10 trillionaires in total.

Fatberg, as everyone called him, though that was not his real name, nor how he looked. First had come the blogs, then the bumper stickers for the gas cars that people then drove, the T-shirts branded with 10k2, and the slogan, 'Ten thousand towers to save the world.' The 10 megathon concerts followed, staged in the parks of 10 great cities in 100 countries. The population of the planet, in relays 10,000 strong holding hands across borders, shouting out 'Ten Thousand Towers To Save the World' repeating the Man's promise to capture the carbon emissions we were all drowning in and convert it to durable consumer goods, designed to be repairable, unlike previously. Too bad none of it had worked, the donations and the songathons of 10,000 stars, though admittedly the majority were not stellar, with billions joining in. Most of the towers were crumbling now. Too much sand in the concrete, not enough grit in the mix. Insider blogs, inevitably taken down soon after they were posted, told of shady deals behind the scenes, poor working practices, flaws in the construction, the deaths hushed up. All in all, the ten thousand towers were a fitting memorial to the vain egos of the many, to believe that climate change initiated three centuries before, when the wrecking ball of the Industrial Revolution got rolling, could be so swiftly reversed. That was in the Enlightenment, Jake remembered, when the tyranny of kings ended and faith in the old religions was eclipsed by the new belief in scientific progress and rational thought. Louis XV got his head chopped off in the same hour, possibly the same minute, that Vesuvius had erupted in Italy. A fact that had always struck Jake as strange. Europe was on fire, armies marched, Royalists and Republicans clashed, Beethoven composed his 5th, Napoleon invaded Russia. All was ferment. There never had been a time like it since…

Not since Prometheus had stolen fire from the gods in Olympus and given it to mankind. He had taken pity on them, because they were cold. Of course, everything then went wrong and a lot of things got burned, a cycle of destruction which still continued to this day.

Jake laughed, thinking of the Greek legends his grandfather had read to him when he was a child. Always beware of Greeks bearing gifts his grandfather had said, closing the picture book with a snap, patting him on the head and holding up a finger to point to where the gods lived and to his bedroom in the attic, which was a Greek word, his grandfather said, as he sent the boy to bed.

In the story, Zeus sentenced Prometheus to ten thousand years for his crimes, which were two, but the second was worse. Cast down from Olympus like Lucifer into Hell in the Bible story, Prometheus was chained to a rock, where by day he had his liver torn out and eaten by an eagle, only for it to regrow each night. Ten thousand years. As a child, Jake often thought about his suffering. A black eagle, its great wings blotting out the sky as it descended. The terror and torment. The sharp claws, tearing and ripping. Then the same the next day. More than a hundred lifetimes. How must Prometheus have cursed humanity who, in the legends, he shaped from clay and animated with his breath. Our spirit, his breath, our madness his madness. Crazy fuckers all, when you got down to the bone. Like father like son.

Ten thousand years ago, looking down on the fires from Olympus, the gods must have thought much the same. Perhaps that wrecking ball had been the measure of Prometheus's hatred for all that time served and his revenge on ungrateful humanity? Beware of Greeks bearing gifts. Progress, what progress? Three hundred years since the Industrial Revolution and the population of the world had gone from five hundred million to ten billion, and the planet was burning.

Could the climate really be turned round in one generation, as governments and the green corporates insisted, holding up the carrot of ever-renewing electricity? That was a laugh, with the long smog now rendering the photo-voltaic cells of the sun farms north and south inoperative, but for a narrow band around the desertifying tropics, without which the lights would have gone out. Wind farms fared no better, the climatologists now saying that within 30 years, mean wind speeds could be approaching that of Venus, where the cyclones regularly exceeded 800kph, forcing us all to live underground in order to survive.

Hubris had got humanity its reward with a busted flush. And all the time Fatberg and his pals sucked in the credits and plaudits instead of being hanged drawn and quartered, their heads spiked on the towers for their numerous crimes. Still selling believing fools short with FakeReal dreams – including himself, Jake reflected, wryly – as they were monitored day and night, confined like the rest of the population in stuffy apartments behind sealed windows that were never opened for fear of long-dormant viruses lurking in the smog.

Unnoticed, the sweep of the second hand of his watch marked his two minutes roof time as up.

Jake Cousins' reverie was interrupted by a sudden thrumming that intensified with a whirring of multiple rotors, a super 8 predator WatchGog, its telescopic arrays fully extended, the C90 bucky balls of its iridescent carapace proof against any projectile short of a direct strike by stinger missile, a miracle of captured carbon. The promised dividend of the Towers, turning transparent in the sun, made the drone appear like a giant antediluvian dragonfly roused from a long Siberian sleep. It rose out of the fog, 50 yards to his left over the parapet.

As it veered towards him, the distorted robotic voice issuing from the super bug's speakers barked its usual refrain.

'Toxic Air Alert, return to your place of shelter immediately. Warning, ten seconds to Penalty Code 307 Violation.' The message repeated, with a final warning abruptly cut off as Jake pulled the open cover of the old ventilation duct back down over his head.

Praying he had made it inside in time, he stepped down into the hall and pressed a concealed button in the wall, the ladder smoothly retracting on its compressed air suspensors, the ceiling panel sliding shut above him, hiding the illegal hatch from sight just as Carrie appeared in the doorway of her workroom, a witch wearing the mask of Hecate and an expression fit to curdle milk. This being just after midday, when she performed her exercise routines, she was wearing her 'Maid Marion' outfit, a vivacious sherwood green leotard from the international dance company's last travelling production, Robin Hood in Tights, which had originally brought her to the City, as he'd only learned much later. It conformed to the curves of her ballet dancer's body so closely that the material seemed painted on, Jake considered, appreciatively, as he braced himself for the inevitable tirade.

'You bastard,' she began.

He shrugged, his gaze sliding over her shoulder, to the winking eye of a V-cam in the darkened workroom behind her.

'Look at me, goddamn it!' Carrie snapped. She stamped a heel. 'You promised.'

'I know, I know.' He hung his head, unable to repress a smile.

'Goddamn it, Jake, must I spell it out? Just two more violations this year and it's off to the camps you go. How long do you think you'd last with the swampies you feel so much pity for, huh?' she choked, blinking back tears. 'And what would happen to me? Without you I'd lose my Guest Status in the City. Do you ever think of that?'

'Of course, of course. But I was half back in the vent when the Gog appeared. Had it covered all the time.' He winked. 'You know me, quick as a fly. Honestly,' he lied, 'nothing to worry about, babe.'

'You shit!' she hissed, more than anything infuriated by his boyish, winning smile. 'Don't think you can sweet talk me round. Every time you go up there, you risk *us* too.'

'Carrie.' Jake pointed up with his thumb. 'Without what that represents to me, I'd go insane trapped down here. Those precious two minutes of roof time I grab are the thin line between me and madness. You know that.'

'All our friends have to suffer the same. Why must you be different? Few if any have an apartment half as big, and none with *views*.' Her pale lips twisted.

'That's what I bought it for, the views. You know that!' he countered, feeling stupid as he said it. Over her shoulder, the papered over windows of the workroom, reminded him of her acrophobia, a fear of heights, and how she stayed arms-length from the walls when the building swayed and echoed with eerie sounds in high winds. Jake had long since grown used to them, hardly heard them in fact as they welled up through the substructure, which was designed to take the strain, as he had often told her. God she was funny sometimes, he thought.

'You bastard.'

'Sorry, that was insensitive. Please let's not fight.' He reached out, withdrew hastily as she slapped his hands away. 'I love you, babe.'

'Don't dare call me that!' she snarled, turning on her heel. She slammed the workroom door behind her, precipitating a light fall of dust from a jagged crack that, unbeknownst to either party, had opened up parallel to the lighting track in the ceiling only that morning, suggesting all was not right with the Pierspoint.

'Love you too. Always, babe,' Jake said, softly, as he stared into what, under the overhead spotlights, seemed like a swirl of diamond dust swept up in her wake.

As Harry, the auto-vac they had named after a pigmy elephant at the City Zoo (which had died tragically at the start of the Emergency and flitted amongst the FakeReal headlines for weeks), emerged from its hatch in the wall, its proboscis wavering in the general direction of the offending dust, Jake retreated into his study.

Ignoring the glowing display demanding his attention, illuminated in black light under the open hood of the Verity Console, he picked up the sound remote on his desk. Jake coded in the Ride of the Valkyries and turned up the volume. Wagner usually did it for him when he was in this mood.

Outside the windows, the smog was back, its eerie light filtering through grimed glass, showing up all the streaks of seabird shit and dirt deposited in the endless shut-in, making him feel like he was weighed down by an iron aqualung, trapped in a diving cage, 10,000 fathoms deep, instead of 22 floors up in an apartment that was the envy of all his chums.

Peering into the Pleistocene gloom outside the windows, he wondered if he had plumbed the depths or his descent had just begun. Sink or swim, what choice was that when the pressure was 10,000 millibars and rising? How long before the iron lungs strapped to his back imploded?

He jerked round as the door was flung open behind him.

'What?' he exclaimed. She had changed from Maid Marion to Ms Goody business suit. Now her blonde hair was drawn in a tight bun at the back of her head, instead of loose as before, her peacock blue eyes luminous behind the chunky black frames of her spectacles.

'Turn the sound down,' she yelled, 'I'm expecting an important call!'

'Obviously, dressed in those pinstripes, with your boss face on,' he shouted, picking up the remote from his desk. 'Who is it this time?' He shut the Valkyries off mid-ride.

'Fatberg for all I know,' she laughed. 'He hides behind a mask and stays behind a huge marble desk. And he's got big French windows open behind him, onto a meadow dotted with flowers.'

'Switzerland?' he guessed. 'One of those Alpine haute canton condos of the super-rich, d'you think? No yodeling, grazing cattle with bells tinkling, or watchtowers and robot guards patrolling in the distance, I suppose?'

'Well, the mountain in the background did look familiar,' she laughed.

'The Matterhorn?' he hazarded.

She shook her head. 'More like Katchajuga, in the Caligooga Range.' She looked away, remembering. 'Yea, where I used to go camping in South Island with my dad, as a kid.

'Probably fake but you never know,' she went on, after a moment. 'The pixel count was off the scale on my feed, and when I played the recording back, it was scrambled, which has got to mean something.'

He raised an eyebrow quizzically, then held up a thumb and forefinger and rubbed them together.

'We'll see,' she shrugged, always tight-lipped about her corporate clients. 'I have high hopes with this one. And how's your work going, Sir Parcival?' She nodded towards the V-Console and a stack of shimmering squares, defined by myriad glowing lines, under the hood.

'Okay, just tidying some floor plans on the CAH.'

'Not still on those new subs they're planning for the abandoned Firebrick Estate?'

'That's the one.' He sighed. 'Hell, If I wasn't doing it, someone else would be.'

'Like laying out the designs for Dachau.'

'I sincerely hope not.' He spread his hands. 'But what choice do I have?'

'None of us do.' She nodded. 'Perhaps below ground will be an improvement for the swampies. At least it should be dry down there. God knows it must be murder in the camps.'

'Literarily,' Jake added.

'Yes, and with dengue and malaria endemic, confined ten to a hut, no air-con, as you were about to remind me.'

'Don't forget the lack of filters in the inadequate ventilation, and the Siberian shit wafting through holes in the roof and leaking through the broken window seals.'

'Horrible, I agree! But what is the point of beating your drum when there is nothing you or I can do? Work, and work alone, will keep that Gog from our door,' she said, forcefully. 'Unless of course you want to take the Universal Credit option like your swamp bait drinking buddies,' she added, with a NZ twang.

'Not all of them are on Bred,' Jake said, hotly, referring to the Basic Real Ethical Dividend which, three years into the Emergency, most people got by on. 'But you're right.' Sighing, he glanced at the glowing hologram in black light under the console. 'I need to get those plans off before the five o'clock deadline, otherwise I won't get paid this week.'

'That's my boy.' Alerted by a sudden ping, she looked down at the display of her smartwatch, which had lit up. 'Shit.' She frowned. 'Would you believe it! That was from the Man in the Mask's appointments manager, wanting to reschedule today's session!' She started towards the door, stopped, smiled and said, 'Oh, and I'm not making supper tonight.'

'How do you figure that? It's your turn. I was quite looking forwards to your Friday paella,' he protested.

'You earned the forfeit with your performance fiddling on the roof earlier,' she laughed, before closing the door softly behind her.

Supper that evening was a simple meal. Necessarily, because Jake was responsible. But Carrie said it was good, and she was a great cook, so Jake took it as a compliment.

Yet he was still peckish after finishing his portion of croquettes, microwaved cauliflower florets sprinkled with cheese and breadcrumbs and torched by the flame wand, and steamed asparagus tips, also from the freezer. In total the meal came to 1280 calories, of which Jake consumed approximately 60%, his portion being that much larger than Carrie's as was customary between them. Though he resented her controlling ways when it came to calories and cuisine, he realised her strict dietary regime kept him fit and lean.

He also appreciated his leash being loosened on Friday nights, for his weekly blow-out. And if she offered the occasional comment on his inebriated state when he crawled into bed, he always had the examples of those buddies who had ballooned in the Emergency – more to the point, his parents and their relationship. His father had loved a fry-up, and his mother believed in filling her man with comfort food. Both had died in a head-on car crash, the two joyriders walking away with minor injuries and some community work in an old folks' home. It was a judgment which still enraged him, though his father could have gone any time from a massive coronary, his arteries choked by cholesterol as the medical examiner of the life insurance company later reported, information that didn't come as a surprise to Jake.

On his last visit to his parents, he had seen the signs in his father's flushed face: the prominent vein pulsing ominously on the bridge of his nose, the burnt look of his cheeks, the skin crazed by broken capillaries like baked mudflats when the sun is sinking into the horizon and the tide has run out. His mother he didn't miss much; they'd never really got on.

His only sister was ten years older and had been more like an aunt when he was growing up. He'd still been in high school when she got religion and hooked up with a crazy Baptist preacher, who his father called

Holy Joe, and turned her back on the family. Last he heard she had three kids and they were living in a trailer park somewhere down south, where Holy Joe ministered to his flock of white trash in his church in a shipping container.

Jake had left home at just 17 to seek his fortune, which finally found him in Carrie. And so his connection with his parents, apart from the occasional flying visit – literally, because the journey was 3000 miles diagonally back across the vast country – consisted of a birthday card with a printed message, co-signed with the ritual XXX from Mom, and at Christmas a joint phone call that went on for about five minutes. That was about the sum of it. But his father was a big loss. Too bad the old soak, who was a big sports fan and liked a drink when he watched games, didn't live long enough to meet Carrie. That was one of the sadnesses. Jake was sure they would have gotten on.

After the meal, Carrie helped him clear-up, which was a big concession because the rule was whoever cooked then cleaned the plates, before loading them into the dishwasher. But it was his night with the boys, and she didn't want him to be late. Six days a week they took turn and turnabout, and on the seventh, Sunday, they ordered in from a premier whizz that guaranteed its ingredients and had an accredited 5-star trust rating, which was important with ongoing disruptions to the supply chain and food shortages. As per their agreement, there was a set menu for each day, and a recipe book to hand that Carrie had typed up for when Jake needed it.

Yes, she was a tyrant, but only relating to matters of diet and cuisine. Otherwise, domestically, it was pretty much give and take. But in bed, it was a different picture altogether, with Jake expected to take the lead, which suited both just fine.

The day they collided – as the clock in nearby City Hall chimed midday, he'd been jogging round a street corner, and she had been coming the other way, shopping in a new outfit of green silk, her high heels clicking the sidewalk.

After he picked up her frayed jeans, blouse, and old trainers strewn across the sidewalk, stuffed them back into the dropped carrier bag where they had been bundled, and apologized profusely, she'd gracefully accepted his invitation for a coffee. In the shaded light of the café, their heads close over the table furthest from the street window, he couldn't decide whether her wide set eyes above perfect cheekbones were green or blue, but settled on the latter. Their hue, he finally decided, was the same iridescent blue of peacock feathers.

They lunched at the Old Pier Bar, a personal favorite of Jake's. She took her heels off and went barefoot as they walked to the end of the long stone pier, half circling the original harbor, where Jake slipped an arm around her waist as he pointed to distant features around the bay. She said it was her day off, without specifying from what or whom, he replied he had nothing pressing and suggested a leisurely stroll along the promenade by the foreshore.

It was 5 o'clock when he hailed a cab and, after another coffee which neither finished, they went to an early show in the theatre district. Looking back, he never could recall the title, nor what the play was about, probably because his attention was so completely focused on her.

Much later, they fell into bed back at his place, and she stayed. Everything was so natural between them over the following days that he never questioned what was already implicitly a permanent arrangement, even though he still knew next to nothing about her.

He found he liked the mystery of not knowing who she was and where she came from. Though blonde like all his former girlfriends, she was different to all of them, and he wanted to keep it that way.

But despite that, Jake was unable to restrain his curiosity when her diary fell onto the hall floor from an assortment of her bagged possessions, as he was moving them into his Pierspoint apartment.

The pretty little book had padded pink calfskin covers and a tiny gold key on a fine chain, also of gold, still in the lock of its ornate golden clasp. He supposed that in the haste of the move from the Apart Hotel (again no explanation why there, when real apartments were so much more affordable) she had forgotten to lock the diary and remove the key.

Seeing that the book had fallen open at the last entry, coincidently the very day they had met, Jake couldn't help looking closer (nor feeling that he was a wretched sneak). Still, he read what was written, in her elegant flowing hand.

Today is about Hair and Him. he read. *I have the surest feeling this is the day that was promised in the pact I made, so long ago it seems, but only a year ago in fact, when I decided to get my genes tweaked with all that money Dad left. I wonder what he would think of my new blonde hair, which at last has grown out and is only black at the tips where they touch my shoulders. So it's off to the salon, where I'm booked in with Kenny, to finally cut them off for Mr Right (who prefers blondes, I know, because the VOICE told me!) then a new outfit for the new look to go with the hair, and then!***!!!*

Jake was shocked. He felt sick, confused, but most of all a sense of having been tricked. What and who was this 'pact' with? And that 'Voice' was too spooky to be true. But in a way he felt flattered she would spend her inheritance on fixing herself up at some clinic for Mr Right - yes, him.

But goddamn, he still felt conned and manipulated. This Carrie Erheart was a gene-edited iteration of the original and therefore a fake. But would he have invited her for a coffee had her hair been a different color? On reflection he doubted it, given that he hadn't completed his midday run. On first sight he had been entranced, because she so fitted his ideal, and that included the blonde hair. So maybe he was a fake too?

Jake never let on that he knew, and she never mentioned the gene therapy or her previous hair colour, which he suspected had been black as pitch, as befitted a witch - *his beautiful witch*.

At midnight, two months after Ms. Carrie Erheart moved in, the Global Emergency was declared by the UN Security Council. It came following a resolution in favor passed earlier that day by an overwhelming majority of nations in an extraordinary plenipotentiary session of the General Assembly. Then, like everyone else, they were locked into the first iteration of a fake world that overnight had become manifestly real.

*

CHAPTER 2

ATMOSPHERIC FORECAST/ SOUTHERN HEMISPHERE,

Conditions are generally fair at altitudes of between 1500-2000 meters with only light particle distribution expected.

Katoomba weather station in NSW reports that particle concentrations are high over Western Australia, due to uplift from the recent sandstorms in the Nullarbor Desert.

Altitudes over 2000 meters should be clear except in countries bordering Equatorial Guinea, where there is a problem with sulphur particulates and ice crystals, circulated by the jet stream, from the super volcano which is still erupting under the sea in the mid-Atlantic trench.

Giant's Castle Weather station, in South Africa, reports swarms of flying insects at 9000 meters due to local drought conditions.

Fatberg, as the genius creator of FakeReal was universally known, was having trouble with his digestion. His real name was Julius Adamos Kyriku, though intimates of his inner circle called him Fats to his face – even though he was anything but. After almost two decades, corporate acquisitions, mergers, and buyouts had raised him to the top of the heap and made him the richest man in the world.

Unlike most trillionaires, Fatberg didn't hail from a privileged background. His parents were Greek, and had come to the country to start a new life. They'd worked and saved hard, pinched the pennies, and thought they had made it big when they paid cash on the nail (all those pennies) for a two-garage house in the suburbs. Nothing special about except perhaps for the strong work ethic they instilled in their gifted only son who, unlike them, was born into a society where most children were kept in a constant state of excitement by sugary confections, placated with treats and entertainments streamed on coast to coast, senators looking down their august noses, judges wearing wigs, historians holding tomes, bishops in skirts with miters on their heads, scientists studying equations in folios, others peering to microscopes, classical composers plucking lyres, writers dipping quills into inkpots, philosophers garbed in sackcloth, pondering skulls – all the Enlightenment archetypes were here.

Perhaps strangely, however, especially considering how the frat house stood out compared to the austere, restrained classical styling of the other stone buildings of the Old Campus, no mention was made of it in the university's guide books. Nor did it come up in the accounts of illustrious former students, eminent scientists, wealthy philanthropists, famous politicians, respected writers – a roll call of the great and good, alumni whose names were embossed in gold in the assembly halls of their respective colleges, lists which included many Nobel Prize winners. Nor was the anomalous building marked on any of the maps handed out to freshers, interested parents, or visiting academics. Indeed, it was as if the frat house did not exist at all.

As previously noted, Fatberg was having trouble with his digestion. Lately, episodes of flatulence had disturbed his sleep, which might have proved embarrassing had Fatberg not always slept alone, preferring his own company to that of others. Recently, his butter-wouldn't-melt-in-the-mouth choirboy face had taken on a lean and hungry look, and his normally clear complexion had a distinct pallor.

Pondering the matter under black light in the special room where he meditated every morning for a strict thousand seconds, suggested that the condition was connected to a certain event in his past – one which he wanted to forget, so that didn't help. Precision timing in all things was a secret of his success, he'd informed his official biographer in their last session, which of course was remote, not least because at any time Fatberg could be in a different high-altitude location in his portable palace, which was a replica of Caesar's palace on the Palatine Hill in Ancient Rome.

Julius was in the dressing room, checking the fit of his mask in the mirror, when he abruptly changed his mind and pulled it off, exposing a grimace. He then spent a full two seconds adjusting the knot of his tie. Since the Emergency, ties were important. Ties projected stability, order, confidence, predictability, that's what people needed now.

What was he thinking? She was only a fucking counsellor.

He removed the tie. Unbuttoned his collar. Leaning close to the mirror and peering into his own pale blue eyes, for the first time in his thirty-eight years Julius saw defeat, and the weights of the world that success and the expectations fuckers everywhere had placed on him. Not the weights – stupid. He shook his head, it was that thing bugging him, again.

What the fuck, he shrugged. He could walk away anytime with a fucking Himalayan mountain range of cash, never look back. Really? That wasn't him either.

What I am, he reminded himself sternly, repeating his old mantra since the frat house, *is no second thoughts, Blitzkrieg, break plates, scorched earth, take no prisoners, donner and blitzen, Lightning strikes. Bam! Bam! Bam! To the victor the spoils and the devil take the hindmost. That's me, yea.*

His guts twisted again. Beware the anger of the gods. Oh yea, his father in his letter before he croaked, going on about hubris.

'Damn him and his investments,' he said out loud.

Simultaneously, the floor under the soles of his immaculate shoes juddered ever so slightly, as with a muffled hiss, the portable palace set down softly in a remote jungle clearing in Ecuador, one of South America's last tranches of undisturbed rainforest, which of course he owned along with the mountain it backed onto. Outside the windows of the dressing room, macaws were cawing and brightly coloured insects buzzed in the trees, as if everything was right in the world, which obviously it wasn't, because he had indigestion.

Right then he decided to face the inevitable and go through with what he knew was going to be a horrible ordeal.

*

Jake (Bonny Boy) was having fun. Real Friday night fun down at the old Warbiton. Shooting the Gog, wagging the chin, exchanging jokes and ribaldry with his buddies. Simon (Griffin) Jay, Walter (Beastie) Potts, Iain (Smurf) Begg, Jim (Dixie) Watts, Gerry (S'nuff) Packer, Harry (Dizzy) Day, Gregorski (the Hat) Kaptcha, Moses (the Prophet) Tyler, none of whom were there.

All were safely shut in, away from the smog, back in their stuffy apartments, drinking from bottles, cans, glasses, instead of the frothing tankards seemingly in Griffin's, Beastie's, Smurf's, Dixie's, S'nuff's, Dizzy's, the Hat's, the Prophet's, and Bonny Boy's hands. Even the Warbiton was not real. Three years before, when the appalling implications of the new Emergency which had just been declared became clear, they'd pooled their credits (the waged chipping in thirty percent more into the pot than those on BRED) and purchased a template pub, which came with a basic barmaid from one of the sites offering virtual environments on the FakeReal.

First off, they'd agreed on the name, then that their pub should provide a total escape from their present situation and should be located elsewhere in time and space. Pub rules were also important; there should be no talk about anything that might divide them, so they ruled out the subjects of women, smog, and the Emergency. After a lively discussion of where to locate the Warbiton they finally settled on London, mid-19th century, a period which though within their cultural parameters was as far removed from the current reality as possible, except perhaps for the persistent fog which writers like Dickens employed to add atmosphere to their novels. After much debate, they agreed the fog could stay, but must remain safely outside the pub windows.

Pooling more credits, they installed Sam, a doorman in appropriate period costume to welcome them in, with a basic vocabulary of fifty words. Next they upgraded the barmaid to buxom saucy maid, gave her a thousand-word vocabulary, much of it coarse such as a working girl of her class and era might be expected to know, and a lively line in chat. That all done they added a snug, installed some dial-up literary characters in case any of them wanted different company or they needed expert arbitration on a moot point in one of their literary pub quizzes.

They then set about furnishing the pub, which again involved much discussion and pooling of credits on successive Friday nights to decide on the choice of furniture, bar fittings, oak beams, nicotine-stained walls, etched mirrors, old paintings, worn floorboards, spittoons, steamed-up windows, candlesticks, a fireplace in a cosy corner with log fire, and all the sundry period things that go together to make the classic Ye Olde English Pub. They researched, saved up for, and then purchased these items – again, only after much debate and visiting of the many sites on the FakeReal offering non-fungible replicas, which in the virtual environment of the Warbiton were real enough to touch. All of which they needed to make a place to feel at home in, far removed from their real homes, where they were shut in for the duration of the Long Smog.

*

Seated behind his desk, Fatberg ran his tongue around his spotlessly clean teeth, grimaced, pursed his lips, and touched his collar, again checking that the tie that wasn't there. Then, with a resolution he didn't feel, he circled his index finger of his right hand in the air, summoning his Appointments Manager, who immediately materialized in micro format before him, projected onto the shiny marble surface of the desk in a beam of black light.

'Yes sir!' the tiny homunculus said, his hands clasped before his waist, standing looking up at Fatberg.

'You can put the call through now,' Fatberg ordered.

The homunculus promptly disappeared in another beam of black light to do his master's bidding. Moments later – exactly ten seconds, Fatberg noted with a slight feeling of satisfaction – the black light was back, this time forming a pane that expanded to the width of the desk, whereupon a seven-eighth size iteration (the maximum permitted callers at the Palace) of Carrie appeared in the frame, also seated behind a desk, only hers was smaller by a factor of ten than his, he noted.

'Fatberg!' she gasped, taken aback. 'But your mask ...'

'Indeed,' he said, his bare face just as expressionless. 'It is I.'

'So I see,' she said, recovering. Then, pointing with the little finger of her right hand, she indicated the picture window behind him, where the sun was setting behind the forested slopes of a snow-capped volcano. 'And you've changed the scenery. Are those macaws in the trees?'

'Yes.' He nodded.

'The Ecuadorian high-altitude rainforest, I suppose?'

'How did you figure that?'

'Ecuador has the highest volcanoes in South America, like that one.'

When he said nothing, just stared, she pointed over his shoulder again.

'The snow on the top.'

'Uh, yea,' he said, checking. He looked back round at her. 'And?'

'It's about the same latitude as where I am.'

'What makes you think that?'

'I can tell from the position of the sun.'

'Amazing.'

'Is it real?'

'Yes.'

'And was your last location, high in the Caligooga Range and looking onto Katchajuga, real too?'

'I hoped you would recognize the mountain,' he said, pleased.

'Frankly, I wasn't too happy, as it told me you've delved rather more deeply into my past than I like.'

'In my position I have to know as much as possible about people I deal with.'

'I see,' she said. 'And now that I know who *you* are, surely ...'

'You knew that already, Counsellor,' he said, leaning forward over the desk, his pale blue eyes intent on the minutia of her facial muscles. His expertise in reading faces was one secret of business success which he hadn't told to his official biographer.

'Well, I guessed,' Carrie said, recovering her poise, every inch of her cool and professional under his searching gaze, as befitted a counsellor with a 5-star trust rating in Visualization Therapy, a new field of clinical psychology which had become fashionable in elite circles since the Emergency. 'How then should I address you?' she said, after a moment. 'Fatberg? Fats?' She paused. 'Or perhaps Julius?'

He pursed his lips. 'No one has called me Julius since my mother passed.'

'Is she what this is all about? If so, Mr Kiriku-'

'Julius,' he interrupted.

She dipped her head. 'Then you've come to the wrong counsellor. I am not very good at mothers. I never knew mine, as I think you already know, Julius.'

'Yes,' he nodded. 'But no, this is about something else.' His pale unblinking eyes were fixed on hers.

Carrie assumed her listening pose, leaning a little back in her chair, clasping her hands on the desk before her, her demeanour calm, receptive, and alert. 'Please,' she smiled, gesturing with an open palm.

Julius relaxed slightly, though still tense. 'This goes to the heart of all I have achieved in life, my global businesses, the FakeReal, everything. Without which, my world...' He paused. 'Our world, I suspect, might be very different indeed.'

'I see,' she said. 'By any chance, does this relate to your time as a student?'

'Yes,' he replied, sitting straight in his chair, his eyes unblinking. 'And I must underline that what I am about to tell you is a matter of utmost confidentiality.'

'Mr Kiriku – Julius,' she corrected herself, taken aback by his sudden vehemence. 'Whatever you care to tell me is fully covered by the conditions of our confidentiality agreement...'

'If anything should leak out...'

'Nothing will, I assure you.'

'It is not you I am concerned about, so much as your partner.'

She sat bolt upright in her chair, barely able to contain her sudden fury. 'I beg your pardon?'

'That's why I rescheduled our meeting to this evening, when I knew he would be occupied and there was no chance of interruption.'

'I see,' she said, coldly.

'Perhaps we should start again, Counsellor. Look, as a man in my position-'

'As *ruler of the world*, you were about to say?' she interrupted, her ire showing in the penetrating brilliance of her blue eyes.

'Hardly.' He cringed, diminished by the sudden reversal in their respective positions, his shoulders slumping as the weights returned.

*

Jake always took last funicular back home after the pub. Outside, waiting all the time in the foggy gas-lit street, Sam would hold open the door, his big pockmarked face creasing as Jake tipped him his customary sovereign, which was excessive, but Jake loved to see the old lag's face light up as he pressed the shiny gold coin, embossed with Queen Victoria's head, into his calloused open palm.

The Doorman's cheery, 'G'noight guv'nor an' a soife return 'ome,' ringing in his ears, Jake entered the station, which conveniently was just a step across the street from the Worthington. Never anyone else around. At the bottom of the stairs, the ticket office had a closed sign in the window. But like magic, the cable car was always waiting for him, the door open, its cheery light spilling onto the platform. No one inside to bother him.

As soon as he was in his seat, the cable car started off, swaying ever so gently, gathering speed. He liked looking down at the city and its gridwork of neon-lit streets spread out like a plaid blanket in the darkness below, the jewels of stop signs flashing at intersections, the red flares of cars speeding away, comets in the night, the stars of lighted windows in the dark squares of apartment blocks twinkling in triplicate as he tried to focus on them before they passed out of sight.

Ahead, the overhead cable stretched into the distance, where the funicular's tall pylons, like a line of broad-shouldered soldiers with the cable strung between them, marched up the steep side of Pierspoint Hill to the terminus just below McReadies Fort at the top. All in all, the journey took fifteen minutes, from start to stop, by which time he had usually sobered up enough to manage the cool walk across the park without too much difficulty.

Of course, none of this was real. The ride was a custom job purchased from Famous Journeys of the World (tm), a niche outfit on the FakeReal, which a client had recommended. Including the extras – the trimmings of the station, city lights, walk in the park, owls hooting in the trees, and the last leg in the Pierspoint – the bespoke package totted up to rather more than Jake had calculated, plus of course the charge every time he used it, which ironically was more than the real ride had cost before the Emergency was declared and the Funicular was shut down. But considering the pleasure he derived from it, the journey was a bargain.

Usually, however, when the big front doors of the Pierspoint loomed out of the gloom, he skipped the last part, which he regretted buying - the tedious ride in the elevator up to his apartment on the top floor. Instead, he stepped out of the black light of the V-Tent and into the games room of his apartment, home at last, the alcohol in his

'Wow you're hot tonight, he panted, his heart pounding as he rolled off, feeling spent. 'That was great.'

'The earth moved, huh?'

'Oh yea!' He smiled up at her.

'Hmm.' She reached down under the covers again.

The second time was more like a battle between Olympians, first she was on top, then he was. So it went, turn and turnabout, her legs in the air, then her hands pressing his head down between them, visions of nameless things dancing behind his eyes, the heat they generated a furnace, her megawatt cunt grinding his ramrod cock deep in her, stella novum bursting in his brain, her mind and body lit up like the Milky Way, then multiple lightning strikes … forking, when at last they orgasmed together, and this time he was really done.

After a while, lying on his back, recovering, he said, 'Wow, you were too hot to trot tonight, that was a fucking gallop!'

'Hmm ...' she murmured, sleepily.

'You were on fire, babe,' he said, noting with satisfaction the flush on her face and neck.

'And you are a brute, my hero,' she breathed happily, her eyes still closed.

Raising on an elbow to look down on her, connecting the dots at last, he laughed. 'And that must have been some session you had earlier, Carrie.' He prodded her with his thumb.

'Hmm ...'

'So who's the client?'

Her eyes blinked open.

'Come on,' he insisted, sensing the wild triumph lingering in the intense blue of her irises.

In a sudden movement, she pushed him over, pulled the covers up over their heads, pressed her lips to his ear, and whispered, *'Fatberg!'*

'I kne-'

Placing her hand firmly over his mouth, she pointed a finger up at the ceiling, above the covers, then in a slashing gesture drew the finger across her throat, shaking her head.

'Uh,' he grunted, getting the message, his incandescent high of a moment before commensurately down-shifting, as he supposed that the slimeball CEO he most detested and blamed for so much had been with her all the time when he was out at the pub, and her triumph was to do with whatever went down in their session.

Wishing that he was richer than the world-fucker, he faked a yawn, rolled over onto his side, stared into space, and pretended to be asleep.

*

Feeling entirely safe, Fatberg proceeded confidently along the smooth path, which he could just make out ahead, like silver gaffer tape unrolling into the darkness. He was glad it was night and not day, because then he'd have to suppress the urge to stop and count the leaves on a tree.

Always, numbers were always clicking in the back of his head. The world over, shut-in billions clicking submit, submit and submit again, ordering in, chatting with bots, confessing to AI shrinks, immersed in FakeReal verities playing in V-tents, in living rooms, bedrooms, cramped hallways, cupboards, and even the huts of swampies, out in the new marshes of the eroded coasts, the revenues of his companies, piling credits to the moon, where Fatberg had a secret base in a crater, one conspiracy theory went. New ones popping up like mushrooms across the FakeReal, meaning more revenues piling in all the time, the zeros totting up, numbers clicking at the back of Fatberg's head.

Yea, the weights, he sighed, stopping as he saw a fork in the path ahead. Which way? Left, he decided, telling himself to turn right on the way back. OnetwoonetwoonetwoTen! he counted, concentrating so his forward right foot stepped on the path on the 'T' each time. OnetwoonetwoonetwoTen! he counted again. This was radical, no fucker around with a v-cam to record a verity of his lips suspiciously moving, prompting more conspiracy theories on the FakeReal. Onetwoonetwoonetwooha!

Thinking he heard a sound, he froze mid-stride, standing poised on one foot, peering into the darkness. Hearing nothing after taking three more forward steps, he relaxed. Panic over, he thought, looking down, realizing the dumb thing was only a fallen branch. Reaching up, safe from the insects he could hear all around him suddenly, he felt with the fingers of his pheromone gloves the splintered wood on the trunk of the tree leaning over the path, where the overhanging branch had broken off. Could have hurt him.

'Stupid fucking tree,' he said, giving it a kick as he passed which, had he been wearing any other trainers, would have hurt. However, these trainers were reinforced at the toes by a special material also used in the construction of Watchgog drones, which instantly hardened upon contact with solid objects and could withstand being run over by an armored tank. Fatberg was very proud of the shoes, even though they had never gone into production because since the Emergency, there was no market for running shoes.

'OnetwoonetwoonetwoTen! OnetwoonetwoonetwoTen!' Ah-hah, another fork in the path, take right this time, left on the way back. Yea! 'And a OnetwoonetwoonetwoTen! Shit, what was that!' He stopped, uncertain, looking about. Doh! Nothing there, apart from bugs buzzing up in the trees. *Fuck them*, he cursed, waving his fingers at them, *can't touch me I've got my gloves on. Spooky fucking rainforest. Make a good verity though*, he thought. Dumb logs turning into evil snakes.

'OnetwoonetwoonetwoTen!' Smart shadows, with secret powers, not dumbass ones like the inky blots in the greater darkness, which were not shadows because it was too dark for that, but instead he knew just dust sliding in his retinas, as he strained to see in the blackness. Yea, like that out of the corner of his eye, slinking behind the tree with the phosphorescent bark. Spooky or what!

'Onetwoonetwoone …' He stopped counting. Before him, the path branched three ways. *Decide, decide. Right left or … Too many fucking choices. Too tired. Yep. Call it a night, this is far enough,* he decided.

Then, half-turning, he stopped, as a strange melody sounded in the trees. 'What the fuck...?' He strained to hear over the bugs in the background. No doubt about it, that was someone playing fucking pan pipes back there in the darkness. Probably following him all the time, creepy fucker.

Well, fuck them, I'll find another way back, he thought, deciding to take the middle path. The fence around the forest was supposed to keep people out, fucking contractor and his useless guards.

'OnetwoonetwoonetwoTen!'

And again …

'Onetwoonetwoo…' Fucking stupid tree root, he cursed, resisting the temptation to kick it, crouching, rubbing his knee, peering into the darkness, listening. Of course no one was following, never was. Duh. Just his stupid imagination.

Wait, was that the tinkling sound of running water he heard up ahead? So *that* was the flutist he'd heard. He laughed. Suddenly, he felt quite thirsty.

Up on the roof, Jake chuckled to himself, remembering the story the two buddies had made up about the imaginary town where they wished they lived, instead of being stuck in the boring suburbs where you needed a car to get to the city and neighbours had big RV motor homes that never went anywhere except maybe to the garage for a service or, if something had happened to their cars, to a supermarket or the mall.

They just sat there under the trees, gathering leaves on top. Griffin and Jake planned to steal one, drive to a desert somewhere and get wasted. They never did, just smoked weed, told each other stupid jokes, and bragged of making it with girls they only fantasied about. That was in their teens before they both straightened up and went to colleges in different cities. But in the years that followed they still kept in touch.

Good thing they did, Jake thought, because he needed him now. But he would have to be careful. First, however, he would have to brush up on his Shakespeare.

*

Still dripping, sitting by the dark pool from which, only a few minutes before, he had been hauled coughing and spluttering, Fatberg regarded his rescuer resentfully.

'Now, tell me truthfully, who the fuck are you and what do you think you are doing here?'

'Señor.' The Indian looked back from under the brim of his straw hat, which he had just replaced on his head. 'I am the protector of the forest, I look after-'

'Well, I own it,' Fatberg cut him off, 'and you have no fucking permission to be here.'

'Señor, I am born in the forest. I am a Waranka, the last of my tribe, I know all the secret ways. There is no fence that can keep me out.'

'Uh huh, well you can be sure I shall have a word with the contractor about that. Now admit it,' Fatberg glared, 'there never was anything apart from you following me, was there?'

'Señor.' The Indian raised a finger. 'If you look up now, you will see the Panther of the Black Moon on top of the rock.'

'Fuck!' Fatberg recoiled in shock. 'I see it. Fuck, those red eyes!' he gasped.

'Señor, that is only the Panther of the Black Moon's earthly aspect. Its double is much more terrible and has marked you, which is not good, because you saw its red eyes. Ah, look now, it is gone behind the rock. But do not worry.' The Indian laid a hand reassuringly on Fatberg's arm. 'It will not cross the water. You are safe here, I promise. I protect you.'

'What with, your fucking flute?' Fatberg cackled, pointing at the wooden instrument in the man's damp shirt pocket.

'I already use it to distract him when he is about to pounce on you in the forest.'

'So I didn't imagine that strange music.'

'Yes, I learn that from my father who is the protector of the forest before me. The tune is only for when it comes down on the night of the black moon.'

'Whatever,' Fatberg said, impatiently. He stood up. 'Well, I'm out-a-here.'

'Señor.' The Indian reached out.

Fatberg looked down with distaste at the man's brown hand on his arm, as they stood together by the dark pool.

'Señor, without a guide you can never escape the forest and the Maze of the Waranka, on the Night of the Black Moon.'

'Look, man,' Fatberg said, remember how confusing the paths were in the dark. 'Don't think I'm not grateful.' He shook off the hand. 'I'll pay you anything to get me out of this fucking maze, as you call it.' He paused. 'Well, anything within fucking reason, man.'

'Señor, I have no need for money. I am the protector of the forest, I care for every creature in it. '

'You do, huh?'

'Yes.' The Indian nodded. 'Even you, with all your riches.'

'What do you know about that?'

'I see your flying palace each time you return. You cannot fool me like you do the others…'

'What do you mean?' Fatberg glowered.

'Señor.' The little Indian man smiled up at him. 'I see you as you are, alone and frightened, it is that simple.'

'Um.' Fatberg was lost for a reply.

'Come, we walk. This way, Señor, I lead you. '

*

Carrie was worried for her man.

3 a.m. in the morning and he was up on the roof again, this time nursing a jealous grudge against Fatberg. As soon as the name had been out of her mouth, she'd known he would take it that way. So stupid to tell him, but in bed Jake had been insistent, and besides, her exultant feeling following the session had been impossible to contain. Yes, pure unadulterated triumph, she admitted, over the crass pleasure she got from seeing the richest man in the world humbled. Even though it was only whispered under the covers, confiding his name had been a breach of client confidentiality, and now she was paying the price of falling far below her professional standards. The worst of it was she couldn't discuss any related matters with him, unless she wished to incur Fatberg's wrath, whatever that might entail, considering his 'Position'.

But didn't Jake understand he was not alone in loathing the man, not least for the damage he had done to relationships between people? Millions did – no, billions, even as they immersed themselves in Fatberg's genius creation, the FakeReal, which they needed to escape the shut-in.

You had to be strong-minded to stop it taking over your life, as it had so many people's. Her friends often complained how their partners never talked at mealtimes or in bed anymore and instead spent their time finger-scrolling, pulling down menus with the clawing command and fast forwarding with the hand pass till they hit something of passing interest, which appeared before them out of thin air, before they were onto the next search, finger popping, clawing, pointing, gesturing into the air with the FakeReal commands, at things only they could see, like they were insane. However, despite their frequent moans on the general subject, her friends, she knew, would be much the same as their partners unless, as per Carrie and Jake's agreement, they had blocked out the FakeReal in the rooms they shared. Ergo, no FakeReal at mealtimes, or in the bedroom.

For those wealthy enough to afford it, full-mode FakeReal came with black light beams and life-size projection (otherwise only possible in the cumbersome V-tents), and not just small panes that only you could see unless the person was right behind you looking over your shoulder. Then, of course, there were all the other AI bells and whistles, most of which the great majority of users never learned about, because there were so many.

*

'OnetwoonetwoonetwoTen! Onetwoonetwoone…'

'Señor, why do you do that?'

'It's a habit, I suppose,' Fatberg replied from close behind, following the little Indian along the narrow winding path in the darkness.

'I think you cannot stop from doing it.'

'Counting? Yes, you are right,' Fatberg said, too tired to deny it. 'Nobody knows but you, and no one would believe you if you told them.'

'Because I am Indian?'

'Well, yes, I suppose,' Fatberg said, embarrassed to admit the truth.

'I think what you count is the bars of your prison …'

'What?' Fatberg snapped. 'Listen here, I own this forest. And I don't have any fucking limits!' Raising a hand, he twirled a finger, forgetting that in the forest, he was unable to summon an employee in a beam of black light to prove a point to a fucking Indian. 'Shit!' he snarled, stuffing the hand back into his trouser pocket.

'Señor, I think that the bars you count are the things you own, and there are so many of them, more even that the leaves on all the trees in the forest, and that is the reason why you are so unhappy.'

They had reached the end of the path. In the clearing before them sat Fatberg's pink palace, puffed-up and tawdry, as it suddenly appeared to him in the half-light of dawn. He turned to thank the Indian – but the little man was gone, vanished as if he had never been.

*

'You are forfeit!' Carrie said, in her white dressing gown, standing with arms folded, one bare foot tapping the boards, watching Jake as he climbed down the ladder.

Fucking Fatberg, Jake silently cursed, unable to even say the slime-ball's name as he stepped down into the hallway, because then the smart fridge, the phone, the smog detectors, the FakeReal sensors and black light projectors, Harry the Vac, the doorbell that no-one rang anymore, and all the other electronic devices in their apartment would pick it up soon as he did, and then Carrie would be forfeit and, at the very least, lose her precious trust status as a counsellor.

She glowered at him. 'That was a lot longer than two minutes.'

'I know.' Jake hung his head, knowing that if he said another word they would argue, and then she'd winkle out that he was planning something, which he couldn't risk, not when the stakes were so high. He looked up. 'So what's the forfeit to be then, darling?' he said, in as neutral a tone as he could manage.

'I'll think of something. Don't you worry! And you can sleep on the sofa!' she snarled. Then she turned away, slamming the bedroom door behind her. *Fucking Fatberg,* she swore, silently, lip-syncing his name behind her hand, knowing that if it wasn't for the confidentiality agreement and all the watching devices in the apartment, they would now be having a decent row, which would clear the air between them. Right then she decided to refuse Fatberg any more sessions, despite knowing from experience the perils of thwarting the desires of rich and powerful men – and he was richest and most powerful of all – in the unlikely event his appointment manager got in touch.

She'd been too hard on Jake, she thought, already regretting claiming the forfeit. But that was too late to change, and besides, she was sure he was up to something, otherwise he'd never have submitted so easily.

*

In his pink palace, Fatberg was raging.

'Fucking protector of the forest... MY fucking forest, mine to BURN if I want. All the forests will go up in smoke anyway, it's only a matter of time. And more smoke to add to the smog will only boost the already fastest-rising asset values on the planet – high altitude real estate, of which I hold the most because I got in early and shut out all those cheap shmucks in the cities – where the asset values are crashing, and I got out early. Hey, strike three for me! I'll blame the fire on the fucking Indians still hiding out up here, despite the Emergency regs relocating them to the coast, so why the fuck not? Fucking horrible rainforest anyway. Then, no more bullshit Panther of the Black Moon, and its red-eyed double. No more maze of the stupid Waranka, fuck them too. Then I'll fix those guard bots to shoot dead that dumb-ass incompetent contractor. Ha ha! Then, nada mas puta problemos para el stupido Ecuadorians!' Fatberg laughed, hysterically.

Twice now, while waving his hands in the air, he'd inadvertently summoned his unfortunate appointment secretary, who he immediately tried to stomp when he arrived in a beam of black light, which of course was impossible because the full-sized version of his now traumatised appointments secretary was elsewhere.

'Stupido Indian telling me I'm fucking counting prison bars. He's sorry for me. ME! Then the butt fuck disappears before I've finished with him! As for this fucking cheap trash pink palace, I'll drop it in that fucking volcano, replace it with a flying Pizza Hut that will serve slices whenever I want and won't stand out like a sore thumb. Anyway, fucking Julius Caesar was a dumb shmuck who got stabbed by his best friend. Thank fuck I don't have any. All grasping cunts. Yea, and biggest one is that cunting counsellor. Yea, I'll see the bitch disbarred, yea, and her fucking partner sent to the fucking camps. Ha hah, that's for starters, then I'll, I'll…'

Catching sight of his reflection, Fatberg stopped mid-rant. He looked around at the trashed room, saw the antique Roman chairs overturned, the shards of mirror scattered on the mosaic floor, the heel marks and scores of his kicks on the ancient Roman wall fresco that Greasy Spic #2 of the Camorra stole from Pompeii on his express order which he never gave ha ha, because he made it in a shielded room, which was reserved for when he wanted no records of his dealings.

No, this was not him. He was legendary for his composure at turbulent board meetings when every other fucker lost their heads. Equally, in moments of high drama, during acquisitions and mergers, he always kept his cool. So why lose it now? It was the weights he imagined as an upturned Himalayan mountain range pivoted on his skull. The highest peak, the name of which he could never remember, because there was no gain to doing so, bearing down with crushing force, which if allowed to continue would compact his genius brain to a pinprick-sized black hole and suck him and his fortune into it, before disappearing into the smog where all those cheap fuckers down there lived …

CHAPTER 3

SMOG FORECAST for the City and the wider Bay Area, today, 5th August.

Smog cover is expected to be moderate, with an upper limit of 1200ft inland with some thinning around the coast from mid-morning, due to the S.E wind, but considerably thickening further out to sea, with an upper limit of 8,000 ft at the Sound.

Maximum visibility ((DBH) at the surface of 10ft to 15ft is expected at noon.

Analysis of the particulate content at 5am, local time, taken at the City Eye monitoring station (see graphs) was Sulphurics 7.2 4 Organics,12.2, Calcium 24.3 with a virus load of 175 PM2.

For the 15th consecutive day, the Health Hazard Warning remains at Code Red.

Yesterday, a further 17 deaths attributed to smog-related conditions were recorded in the City and Bay area, bringing the total since the start of the Emergency to 21006.

While Fatberg was railing at fate in his soon-to-be-trashed portable palace, at a much lower elevation and some eight thousand miles to the north, Jake was keeping up his strike rate on the old-fashioned keyboard.

It was an option he had chosen today rather than interfacing as he normally would with the AI secretary via his deluxe Sanyon Mark 3 headset, because Griffin, who was something of an expert in such matters, had warned that the new headsets could bug thoughts. It was a possibility Jake had discounted at the time, considering Griffin to be a bit paranoid, but now he didn't want to risk it, given what he was planning for the one slimeball he most hated in the whole world.

They were plans he had already set in motion before he finished work the day before when

It was an option he had chosen today rather than interfacing as he normally would with the AI secretary via his deluxe Sanyon Mark 3 headset, because Griffin, who was something of an expert in such matters, had warned that the new headsets could bug thoughts. It was a possibility Jake had discounted at the time, considering Griffin to be a bit paranoid, but now he didn't want to risk it, given what he was planning for the one slimeball he most hated in the whole world. They were plans he had already set in motion before he finished work the day before when, standing in a corner with his back to all the devices in the room, he'd inserted an inch length of thin copper wire, bent 90 degrees at the tip of the leading end, into a tiny slot in the casing of the headset. But he didn't want to think about that, even though he wasn't wearing the A1 headset, which he also used when down at the Warbiton in the V-Tent.

Clients valued industriousness almost as much as the end result, and while his time was supposedly his own as an independent contractor, analysis of the data at the end of the job (in this case the updated specs he was typing up for the new subs on the Firebrick site) sometimes provided almost as much information as the direct and covert surveillance employees and other homeworkers were subject to. However, at least Jake could be reasonably sure that the data relating to that day could not include his innermost thoughts.

Beep. At the familiar sound, Jake looked up as a message flashed across the screen.

STORM WARNING repeat STORM WARNING Strong winds gusting to excess of 190kph are expected in the Bay Area later today. Residents <u>must</u> at all times <u>remain in their homes</u>. If for any reason you are unable to report property damage to City Eye, do not *move from where you are. Await assistance, which will arrive when conditions permit.*

In her workroom, Carrie had seen the same warning and was already trembling head to foot in anticipation. Strong in just about everything except when the high winds came, the building swayed. Her guts had turned to water.

'Carrie, are you ok?' Jake knocked on her door.

'Go away, Jake, you know there's nothing you can do to help.'

'Sure, babe, but call me if you need me, okay...?'

He waited for a moment, listening on the other side of the door, but then after she didn't reply, she heard the sound of his workroom door closing.

Not wanting him to see her weak and pathetic, as she thought of herself when in the condition, she resisted the urge to call him back.

Curling up on her couch, Carrie covered her eyes and tried to wish herself away. Anywhere but on the 22nd floor of a building that, as Jake always told her while doing his idiot best to reassure her, was designed to sway in the fucking wind.

*

Jake had enjoyed working on the subs. It was a good contract that paid well and had plenty to interest him.

There were twelve subterranean levels, interconnected by service lifts, vent stacks, and emergency stairs. The only access was by tunnels, of which there were four. The main one was from the City Eye building, where the homeless would be processed. The warders also entered from there. The second and third led to hubs where food and other supplies were packaged for delivery across the city. The fourth tunnel was reserved for emergency evacuation of personnel, and led to the docks.

Each level could be sealed off from the other floors in case of riot or fire and was designed to house 200 inmates, to be segregated by sex, on different floors. After processing, each inmate would be allotted their own cubicle, which were sound-proofed, and though measuring only 3m x 2m came with shower, wash bowl, shit stool, shelves for personal possessions, and clothes rail, all of which folded away into the stainless steel walls, and from the ceiling, an individual V-tent at the press of a button, hanging over the single bed which converted to a chair.

Each floor also had a well-equipped gym, a sizeable communal eating room, a multi-denominational chapel, a medical ward with beds for 12 patients, and separate rest rooms and offices for warders. Of course, there were many more homeless in the camps out in the swamps that the facility could have housed, but at least it was a start, with nine more subs scheduled for the Firebrick Site before a roll-out of the corporate-sponsored scheme in big cities across the country.

Sometimes, as he worked on the plans, Jake thought he'd be better off in the subs, where at least he'd be able to mix with other inmates instead of being cooped up in the apartment with only Carrie for company. She sometimes drove him crazy despite, or because of, the insane love he had for her.

Outside the apartment windows, the winds increased in strength and, at first almost imperceptibly, the building started its lateral sway. Low groans and strange howls began emanating from the basements, the inner steel structure vibrating along its full length. Carrie was trying not to relive the events of the worst day of her life, when she'd just turned twelve.

The camping trip was a birthday present from John, who everyone thought was her dad. It was a fiction she had to keep because otherwise the people who had killed her real father and mother would find her and John, who had been her father's best friend. As such, he and she were living as father and daughter under assumed names in South Island, New Zealand.

That morning they started out early to climb Katchajuga, and they were halfway up the mountain when the sky darkened and the storm hit. They decided to camp and wait the storm out, but when the winds increased still further, John said they'd better turn back before it got even worse. He was scouting around, looking for an easier route down, avoiding the steep way they'd come, when he slipped and plunged to his death. She knew nothing of that, of course, till after she was rescued an eternity later. Two days which she spent in abject terror, huddled in her sleeping bag in a violently flapping and ripping tent, pitched against the side of a narrow gulley, waiting for the man she called dad to return, which of course he never did.

The raging storm outside the Pierspoint had reached its peak and the building was swaying to the maximum lateral degree its architects had allowed when the smartwatch on Carrie's wrist lit up.

Automatically, without first checking to see who it was, Carrie pressed the tiny button on the side of the smartwatch and took the call.

'Ms Erheart?'

'Yes,' Carrie said, weakly, wishing she hadn't picked up, hardly able to hear the caller at the other end over the eerie sounds the building was making.

'I'm calling to arrange the...' He was briefly cut off as the lights in the room flickered. 'Ms Erheart, are you still there?'

'Uh, yea.'

'Ms Erheart, what are those sounds?'

'It's the... ah, storm. Can you speak up, it's not a very good connection...'

'I see. Well, I'm calling on behalf of …(inaudible)… to arrange the next ...'

'Please get on with it, I'm very busy right now.'

'Sure, Ms Erheart, shall we say next Friday, same time?'

'Yea, uh, whatever…?' At that moment, Carrie would have agreed to anything just to end the call.

Only after there was a click from the other end did she realize the caller had been Fatberg's appointment manager, and she had just agreed another session. Not just a big mistake, it was a trap she had fallen into, she realized with awful certainty, set by someone aware of her condition, and the call had been timed to coincide with the height of the storm, which was now lessening outside. What else, she wondered, with a cold feeling in her stomach, did Fatberg know about her?

'I could get burned for this, you know, as in charred smoking hole left in the carpet, no other fucking trace!' Griffin said, looking down at the innocuous-seeming headset.

'Seriously?'

'Big time!' Griffin shrugged. 'Corporate cops caught you using that?' He pointed. 'Termination! Pweuff!' He snapped his big fingers. 'Never heard of again.'

'So what do you do with it?'

'Ah ha, that's the very word!' Griffin grinned. 'You've heard of...' His voice dropped. 'The ah...' He glanced in the direction of the shed door, which was firmly closed. '...*Shadow Its?*' he whispered.

'You mean ..?'

'Yep.' Griffin nodded, firmly.

'But I thought they were a legend?'

'No, no.' Griffin shook his head. 'That's what the Corporates would have you believe,' he said, picking up the headset and dusting off the visor. 'Fuckers are terrified of It-tech getting out.'

'So, have you tried that?'

'No, no.' Griffin laughed, putting the headset back down on the bench. 'You know me, Bonny Boy.' He shrugged. 'I just like tinkering with shit. Anyway, making an It is far too dangerous.'

'Why?'

'Because of the substance the symbiote takes.'

'From who, exactly?'

'From their maker, of course.'

'Well, you've got plenty substance to lose, *Beef Cake!*' Jake said, with a grin.

Then they laughed, both thinking of their school days, when only Jake could have gotten away with saying that to Griffin's face.

*

In his bed, warmed by the voluptuous, pleasantly scented flesh of a pre-production cyborg sex doll he had been testing out (a next generation Pricilla, currently in sleep mode), Fatberg was dreaming he was surrounded by dead fuckers in one of his new concept cemeteries which, since their launch a decade before, had become the preferred method of commemorating the departed.

The personalised headstones came in a variety of colours, an ever-expanding range of fonts, scripts, and customized add-ons, and were animated and capable of conversation with relatives visiting the gravesides or family mausoleums. These were rented for an annual fee that was tax deductible. Of course the cemeteries were not real, nothing on the FakeReal was. However, viewed from the perspective of a V-tent, the Momento Mori (tm) were a considerable improvement on the original concept, offering as they did real, genuine solace to the bereaved, a beautifully maintained peaceful environment with no graffiti, vandalism, or crack smokers lurking in shady corners, and a clear expectation of life continuing on the far side, though in a more muted form, after the loved one had passed and their remains had been ethically recycled, reduced to constituent elements, and reprocessed by another of Fatberg's companies.

In fact, this was a consolation in itself, knowing that at any moment, the immortal residue of your late grandfather, or other deceased relative, might be passing through your hands in any number of products. However that did not preclude the life eternal promised in promotions on the FakeReal, which of course was conditional on the annual plot rental fees being paid in perpetuity.

Looking for the cemetery gates and the way out of his dream, Fatberg paced between rows of basic package statuary, mostly headstones, interspersed here and there by obelisks and the odd angel. These lit up as he passed with horrible, leering faces, jabbering a thousand dead tongues, demanding the life eternal promised when they signed up to Momento Mori (tm).

Fatberg stopped by an obelisk he was familiar with, remembering that it was only on his insistence that the design was included in The Egyptian Obelisk Collection in the Momento Mori (tm) Winter Catalogue 37. Of pink fungible granite, it was really quite unimpressive, being only a basic package model, a tenth of the height of the premier deluxe model which was a faithful replica of the original. That had been cut by Egyptian master craftsmen from a block of real granite, 105 feet long. Fatberg recalled the designer going into the boring details of its history, explaining how it was floated on inflated goat skins, though Fatberg found that hard to credit, down an African river for 800-odd miles (the exact number the designer wasn't sure of), and erected in a temple paid for by the widow of a real BCE pharaoh.

Then three thousand and one or two years later, again the annoying designer wasn't sure, it was strafed by the Luftwaffe, when the temple was blown up in the only battle of the Three Day World War, which ended just as abruptly as it began. Thereby, it made two more fortunes for Fatberg who, going on inside information provided by an army general belonging to a certain frat society, had bet heavily on that outcome, dumping all his shareholdings and selling out at the top of the market the day before the war started and then, when the market bottomed out the next day, buying low with everything he had and all he could raise. Thereafter the symbol of the 'Obelisk that Survived', became a popular choice with both high and low-end customers, after both the basic package and the premier deluxe replica, complete with tracer bullet marks, were appended to the

Momento Mori (tm) Winter Catalogue 37, before it was released on the 15th of March the next year.

Happily, the plaque at the base of this obelisk was posted with a tattered, yellowing eviction notice which presumably had already been enforced, because the hieroglyphic name of the lessee had since faded to illegibility on the plaque, and no dead fucker leered out and jabbered in the universal lingua franca the dead spoke in the cemetery, which Fatberg somehow understood perfectly.

'Should have paid your dues, dead sucker,' Fatberg laughed, looking around him, knowing that if he started counting the basic package statuary he'd be stuck here for eternity. There was no end to the rows; they stretched in all directions, by which he supposed he must be in the paupers section. Or maybe not, he reconsidered, catching sight of a massive black outline that somehow looked familiar, looming over the shadowy shapes of the headstones in the darkness beyond.

The mausoleum was a unique non fungible, edition of 1. No one else had a mausoleum like it except of course the original tomb of King Mausoleus, a Greek king who for some reason was buried in Turkey back in the day. A useless fact which had stuck in the back of his mind until it popped out that moment. This struck him as curious, as did the fact that the plaque above the arched double doors didn't light up as he approached. No glowing script appeared, nor did any pale spectre step out from inside. Instead, the double iron doors framed by the ribbed stone arch remained firmly shut at the top of the steps. He had hoped for a conversation and the chance to ask for directions to the cemetery gates. But all was quiet as the proverbial tomb, which irritated Fatberg intensely as he waited at the bottom of the steps, counting the seconds, because he didn't appreciate wasting anything that was his, most particularly his precious time...

'OnetwoonetwoonetwoTen! Onetwoonetwo...'

Fatberg stopped counting, as above him the left side door swung back with a horrible loud creaking noise, which he somehow felt was demeaning because the sudden sound made him jump. That wouldn't have mattered if King Mausoleus or some other spooky fucker had stepped out and answered his questions but, again, no mystery lessee appeared at the head of the steps.

Should he knock, Fatberg wondered, standing before the half open door. 'Hello!' he called into the blackness within. 'Anyone there?'

Receiving no answer, an outcome he could have expected given the non-appearance of the mystery lessee, Fatberg stepped inside. Immediately, the great iron door behind him shut with a clang that echoed

'OnetwoonetwoonetwoTen!
Onetwoonetwo...'

on and on as he listened. But even after he could hear no more echoes, he still felt their vibrations continuing through his fingertips suggesting that the mausoleum was vastly greater in size within than without, and in construction resembled a nautilus shell of an infinite number of chambers.

Panicked, Fatberg reached behind him for the door, but there was nothing. No door, no outside wall. Only a velvet blackness deeper than night. An impossible blackness that seemed to contain the sum of all things, because blank faces, vague objects, unknown shapes and unguessable things seemed to swirl in and out of it as he flailed around looking for the door. He still felt nothing – and nothing under his feet either, he realized with sudden terror that sucked the guts out of him and replaced them with a blank void pervading his body and mind, which was a most threatening feeling that seemed to indicate he was about to expire.

But now, just as he felt his self was about to finally leak away through his toes and out of his shoes, he perceived that the absolute dark all around him vibrated more intensely in places, which was strange because that suggested forbidden It-tech was operating in the background. Also he noted there was a different quality to these patches of darkness. Those to each side seemed to be aligned vertically, whereas dead ahead, there were only two patches, one on top of the other, the one on the bottom much bigger.

'Fuck me!' Fatberg exclaimed, as the one on the top seemed to turn around. As he saw two red dots materialize in the upper part of it, he realized he was back in the middle of the maze of the Waranka, but this time without the Indian guide to protect him, and those burning dots were the malevolent red eyes of the double of the Panther of the Black

Moon, which suddenly became a whole lot bigger, as the monstrous beast leapt from the black rock at the center of the maze and descended upon him, its massive jaws wide, horrible teeth bared, and huge claws extended.

*

CHAPTER 4

ATMOSPHERIC FORECAST/ NORTHERN HEMISPHERE,

Friday, 13 August:

Currently at the lower end of its altitude band, at between 5.2 -5.9 miles high, the jet stream will push south from Friday and clear away the low pressure system from Central Europe, bringing settled conditions above the persistent low-lying smog at altitudes over 1200 meters in the Swiss Alps, where there is only light snow cover on the highest peaks.

In contrast, a low pressure system is still firmly in charge in a large area extending from the Caucuses in the west to the Hindu Kush and the Karakum Mountains in the east, where unseasonal snowfalls will continue and are expected to be heavy today on north-facing elevations above 8,000. Further East, the persistent drought continues on the Tibetan Plateau, where erosion is a serious problem. The recent high winds in the region (which are unusual for this time of year) and consequent uplift of dust have added to the already high particulate count in the upper atmosphere to the south over the Indian sub-continent, resulting in cool conditions over the south-facing elevations of the Himalayas, bringing an early start to the annual monsoon with heavy rain expected today at altitudes lower than 2000 meters, where flash flooding will be a serious problem and pose a serious threat to life.

Elsewhere, the recent global cooling trend, attributed to the persistent smog cover in the altitude band of between 0m – 800m over the Northern Hemisphere at latitudes above 15 degrees, continues, with early snowfalls at altitudes over 2500 meters in North America, from latitude 58 in the North to latitude 40 in the south west, with snow expected as low as 750 meters in the western states later today.

Oooohhaaaahhh! Fatberg suddenly awoke beside a next generation Pricilla, who fortunately was still in sleep mode and so not able to enquire in soothing tones what ailed her lord and master, and try to mollify him from her vast repertoire of sexual caresses and therapeutic techniques.

Just as well, because any intervention at that moment might have induced a heart attack. As it was, Fatberg, who was sitting bolt upright in bed, clutching his chest and struggling to breathe, was still seeing the Black Panther of the Moon descending on him and ripping his palpitating heart out with its massive black claws, a detail of his dream that was to stay with him for the rest of the day.

First thing he did, as soon as he had recovered sufficiently, was jab the index and middle finger of his left hand three times in the air and summon his operations manager, in a beam of black light, to the bedside.

It was embarrassing but had to be done. No matter his reputation for never countermanding an order, this was one he had to change with immediate effect. After the fucking dream, who knew what consequences might result from burning down the rainforest where the evil panther lived when it was not on the far side of the moon. The fucking Waranka and el stupido Protector of the rainforest were welcome to their maze, he decided. Just so long as they kept that evil fucking black panther well away from him.

The order duly rescinded, and feeling a bit more in command of his destiny, Fatberg then set about reordering his day into better shape.

First up was breakfast of sago fruit and buckwheat muesli (which his dietician had advised prolonged life), followed by two tianeptine nootropic pills designed to brighten his mood and reduce stress, swallowed down with oxygen-infused organic orange juice. Feeling a little better, he scanned the financial digest his team had prepared with graphs showing the share price movements of his many companies, as well as those of their competitors and potential takeover targets. The daily atmospheric forecasts came next in his order of priorities, not least because of his interest in adding to his already considerable portfolio of land at higher altitudes.

He had determined that before long the world would be divided by wealth into lower and higher altitudes, with the rich on top and the rest confined to foggy bottom in the depths of the smog, where there was an ample supply of habitable land, in complete contrast to higher altitudes where the law of diminishing supply and increasing values pertained.

Sipping his oxygen-infused orange juice, he then scanned the last item, which only then had popped up in his breakfast table screen. The report, which was from his investigation team, seemed to please him greatly, for he was smiling broadly when he rose from the breakfast table and stepped over to the window.

Outside, his new portable residence was parked next to the Portable Pink Palace – well, in name it was a Pizza Hut, the famous brand logos prominent above its entrance and log cabin finishing on the exterior walls, but it was on such a grandiose scale it more resembled a timber-clad half-scale Coliseum than anything else. Certainly, there had never been a Pizza Hut like it, which together with its colossal size was for Fatberg the main point. Happily, the operations manager reported that the Pompeian frescos were already installed in the al fresco dining room, and the rest of the Pizza Hut was also suitably furnished according to specifications which Fatberg, who didn't want to waste further time on such details, had already laid down. So, all that was left was for Fatberg to familiarise himself with the controls.

That done, he tested its flight capabilities, flying low and fast, skimming across the rainforest, checking for himself that his original order to burn it had indeed been rescinded, and that the contractor was not setting fires along its western perimeter.

Thus reassured, he then took the Hut up to 17,000 feet and parked it 992 feet directly above the volcano. Then he set the geocentric gyroscopes to automatic, ensuring it stayed in that position while he remote piloted the Pink Palace, now empty of its furnishings except for the Pricilla still in sleep mode in his bed, as per his instructions, in an angular ascent, from the jungle clearing 5000 feet below, till it was 200 feet directly below the Pizza Hut. Then he dropped it, straight down, into the smoking cone of the volcano.

Picturing the shop-soiled Pricilla's sudden rude awakening in the bed, Fatberg laughed uproariously, as he watched the pink palace splash down and burst into flames, the tension of his horrible dream at last draining away as his former residence slowly sank and finally disappeared into the smoking magma of the caldera.

Feeling a whole lot lighter, he then manually piloted his new Pizza Hut N-NE towards his next destination, which was located exactly on the Tropic of Cancer at an altitude of approximately 12,000 feet in the Sierra Madre Occidental. He had acquired the hidden canyon in part exchange for a warehouse of used 3rd generation Pricillas and a squad of ex-Israeli army assassin bots, in a deal facilitated by a Swiss intermediary with the Mexican Matuala drugs cartel. They were diversifying out of narcotics which, since the Emergency, had become a lot less profitable, mainly because Fatberg's immersive verities on FakeReal were proving far more addictive than any drug or indeed any combination of drugs to billions of shut-in consumers around the globe.

As the Pizza Hut sped north and he contemplated the smog blanketing the Caribbean coastline of Costa Rica 28000 feet below, Fatberg found himself rather looking forwards to his next session with the counsellor later that day, instead of dreading it as he had been up till then.

*

Breakfast that morning in apartment No 213b, on the 22nd floor of the Pierspoint, was a fraught affair. Jake had already snuck out for his morning two minutes of roof time and was fully dressed, while Carrie was still in her dressing gown. Both apparently were preoccupied with their FakeReal devices, which was against their agreed house rules and certainly not normal behaviour at breakfast.

They sipped their coffees at opposite ends of the hand-crafted maple-wood table, which seemed considerably longer than usual that morning whenever either party snuck a glimpse at the other at the far end. In the hall beyond, Harry the Vac was dallying close to the kitchen door, employing his long trunk-like proboscis somewhat less efficiently than usual, taking his time sucking up the last of the dust which, overnight, had fallen from the long crack in the ceiling above.

'You seeing that same client today?' Jake asked, unable to maintain the pretense any longer.

Carrie looked up from her handheld. 'You know better than to ask about my clients, Jake.' She glared.

'Sorry, I was just wondering, that's all.'

'Well wonder about something else,' she snapped.

He decided against mentioning the forfeit, knowing that to do so would trigger a blazing row – the last thing he could afford, today of all days. Jake grinned back at her.

'Too much work for that today, babe.'

Standing up, he walked around her chair to the open dishwasher and slotted his cup and plate, with a few crumbs of toast left from the one slice he allowed himself before midday, into the top tray. Turning around, he squeezed her shoulder and mussed her hair, which he knew she hated.

'See you later.' He smiled into her eyes,

stealing a kiss before she could avert her face.

'What are you doing out here, Harry m'boy?' Jake said, stepping round the auto-vac outside the kitchen door. 'If I didn't know better I would think you'd been listening.'

Raising his trunk in salute, Harry the Vac pivoted on his casters and watched Jake cross the hall, enter his room, and close the door behind him. Things were not good between his master and mistress, he was now sure.

Seated at his work console, Jake switched on the holographics display and, selecting his pen tool, sketched in a small change where the drain outlets ran into the ventilation stack on the top level.

Satisfied the changes were now duplicated on all twelve levels, he put on his headset, switched to visor display, and felt with his thumb and index finger for the end of the wire sticking out below the visor socket, which he gave a half turn. As he expected, the display dimmed slightly, telling him it was now on reserve battery power. Then he looked up at the menu on the top bar, blinked twice, and when the voice command appeared, said, 'Confirm changes.'

Immediately, his AI secretary replied, in a much scratchier version of Carrie's voice,

'Changes instituted, do you wish to proceed?'

'Yes,' he answered, having also confirmed to himself that the wire he had inserted into the headset the night before worked just as he intended. Then, after saving the changes he'd made to the holographic schemata and double checking, he twisted the wire back a half turn, resetting the headset to main power again, and observed the display brightening as he did so, before he twisted the wire forwards a half turn once more. Finally, having done all he could to prepare the headset for his Friday night session with Griffin at the Warbiton, he switched it off.

*

'Good evening Mr Kyriku,' Carrie said, coldly, as Fatberg appeared behind his marble-topped desk, which seemed to have got larger since the last session.

'Please call me Julius,' Fatberg said, smiling at his max setting of 5.5 insincere warmth.

'As you prefer, Julius.' Carrie nodded. 'I am sorry to have to tell you-'

'So formal this evening, Ms. Erheart!' Fatberg interrupted. Swivelling in his new throne, he indicated the panoramic window behind him and the view of canyon walls turning red by the setting sun. 'I had hoped you might comment on my new location.'

'Mexico is it?' Carrie said, dryly.

'How very astute. Though how you guessed I have no idea.'

'The Mexican flag, hanging from that pole to your left there.' Carrie pointed, aware that she was being diverted.

'So there is.' Fatberg turned back round to face her. 'How very observant of you.'

'Mr Kyriku…'

'Call me Julius, I insist.'

'Julius.' She grimaced. 'I am sorry to have to inform you this will be our last session.'

'I am going to pretend I didn't hear that.'

'Frankly, Julius, I am surprised you would even wish to continue.'

'And *I* am astonished – why do you say that?'

'Well, the lack of progress for one thing. Normally with clients there is only one preparatory session, however we are still at that stage after three sessions. I would have thought in your position-'

'My position!' Fatberg laughed. 'I had hoped we had gotten past that, Ms Erheart.'

'Allow me to reframe that.'

Fatberg nodded. 'Go on.'

'With all the demands on your time …'

'My time is my own to do with as I wish, Ms Erenberg, and I wish to continue.'

'I am sorry but I have made my decision,' Carrie said, feeling her face had gone quite red.

'Ah, I had so hoped you wouldn't say that.' Fatberg smiled at a lower setting.

'It is a question of client counsellor compatibility, Julius,' she insisted.

'I disagree strongly, Ms Erheart, I think we are perfectly matched. So much so that I wish to book your services for a full course of seven sessions.'

'I am sorry, Julius, but that is impossible.'

'My dear Ms Erheart, the word does not exist in my lexicon.' Raising a finger, he sighed, 'I had so hoped not to have to do this, but unfortunately you force my hand.'

With that, Fatberg brought his hand down in an overdramatic gesture and pressed a button on his desk. Immediately, a legal-looking document, headed by the icon of a lidded eye, appeared in a pane before Carrie.

Fatberg went on, 'You will see it is a charge sheet giving the dates and times of twenty-three Penalty Code 307 violations incurred by Mr Cousins in the past six months. It is a considerable list, Ms Erheart, when one considers that just three violations within the period is enough for an immediate transportation order to be served.'

'How did you get this?' Carrie demanded.

'I am not at liberty to say, Ms Erheart. Fortunately, however, I do have some influence with the city authorities, and while I have not been able to persuade them to drop the charges, they have agreed to suspend them. Of course that is, ah, dependent on our relations continuing on a mutually amicable basis.'

*

In FakeReal-time at the Warbiton, Jake (Bonny Boy) and Griffin were reminiscing in the Snug.

'To better times.' Griffin said, raising his tankard.

'I'll drink to that,' Bonny Boy agreed, topping up his tankard and clinking it against Griffin's.

For a moment both buddies remained silent, then Bonny Boy grinned. 'Hey, remember that trick you used to perform at parties?'

'Which one?'

'Yea, you did have a few,' Bonny Boy laughed. 'I was thinking of the handkerchief you pulled through your ears. You never did tell me how you worked that.'

'Nothing to it, Bonny Boy. Apart from skill.' He winked. 'The essential elements are two fleshtone earplugs with tiny hooks in each that catch onto button holes in the corners of two identical white hankies hidden behind my hands. These are tied at the other ends to elastic armbands concealed up my sleeves. When I move my hands back and forth at the sides of my head, the cloth seems to be passing through my ears.'

'Ah, so that's how it's done.'

'As I said, nothing to it.' Griffin shrugged. 'Simple.'

'Then, if you remember, having demonstrated you had nothing between your ears, we followed that with our favourite mastermind game. I asked the questions and you never got an answer wrong, I recall.'

'I always enjoyed showing up all those smart asses.' Griffin grinned. 'It was good for impressing girls too.'

'Shall we play it again?'

'I'm good to go now, if you are.'

'Ok. "To be or not to be, that is the question."'

'Oh come on,' Griffin groaned. 'Hamlet, who else.'

'Just testing you, that's all.'

'Give me something more obscure.'

'"That which I wish to discover, the law of friendship bids me conceal."'

'Better.' Griffin nodded approvingly. 'Ah, I have it, that's what's-his-name, yes, Proteus, the Duke of Milan in Two Gentlemen of Verona.'

'"There are more things in Heaven and Earth, Horatio, than are dreamt of in your philosophy!"'

'Hamlet, again.' Griffin sighed impatiently. 'Come on, hit me!'

'"God made him, and therefore let him pass as a man."'

'Now that is tricky.' Griffin frowned.

'I think I've got you there.' Bonny Boy chuckled.

'No, I have it. Prospero, in Act Five, if I am not wrong.'

'Correct on both counts. See if you can get this one. "This thing of darkness I acknowledge, mine."'

'Ah, one of my favourite lines. The Merchant of Venice.'

'"A horse, a horse, my kingdom for a horse."'

'Too easy! Richard III.'

'Well, horses for courses, when in need, etcetera.'

'Now that is not from Shakespeare, Bonny Boy.'

'I was just saying. See if you can get this. "I can call spirits from vasty deep."'

'That, Bonny Boy, is Glendover, the part I played in Henry the Tit, speaking to Hotspur, who you acted in the play at school.'

'And Hotspur replies?'

'Oh god,' Griffin groaned. 'That was your part, how am I supposed to fucking remember. Oh!' He grinned. 'I have it, "Why so can I."'

'And?'

'It's your fucking line.'

'"Or so can any man ..."' Bonny Boy prompted.

"I have it – and then he says, "But will they come when you call them?"'

'Oh, finally!' Bonny Boy groaned, theatrically.

'I still got it,' Griffin protested.

'And this one I have saved to the last, "It is shaped Sir, like yourself, and it is as broad as it has breadth, it moves by its own organs. It lives by that which nourishes it, and the elements once out of it, it transmigrates."'

'Now that is truly fucking obscure. I'll have to think more on that and get back to you with the answer later. By the by, Bonny Boy, is something up with your headset, your voice has been very scratchy all evening.'

'Yea, Griffin, it's been playing up the past few days. Fucking visor display flickers too. I'm going to have to buy a new one, once I get paid next week.'

'What model do you have?

'A Sanyon deluxe Mark 3.'

'Yea, I know the model. Not the best quality. I have a spare one I never use. You'd be welcome to it.'

'Really? That would be a great help.'

'No worries, I'll send it over by secure-bot once I get over my hangover tomorrow. Now what was my score?'

*

CHAPTER 5

SMOG FORECAST for The City and the wider Bay Area today, Tuesday 10 August.

Smog cover is expected to be particularly dense with an upper limit of 1500ft inland with little or no thinning around the coast until later in the afternoon, when the light wind is expected to switch direction to the SSW, allowing the possibility of some breaks in the smog cover.

Maximum visibility ((DBH) at the surface of 8ft to 12ft is expected at noon.

Analysis of the particulate content, at 5am local time, taken at the City Eye monitoring station (see graphs) was Sulphurics 9.4 Organics,11.01, Calcium 28.2 with a virus load of 202 PM2.

For the 3rd consecutive day, the Health Hazard Warning remains at Code Red.

Yesterday, a further 24 deaths attributed to smog-related conditions were recorded in the City and Bay area, bringing the total since the start of the Emergency to 21168.

For days following the session, Carrie thought she would burst, but now she was used to not being able to offload about Fatberg, and in a way she resented Jake his ignorance of the fact and his free and easy ways.

His daily so-called two minutes up on the roof, which of course he stretched, which had cost her so dear. His Friday nights with his buddies, drinking at their ridiculous non-existent fake tavern. She didn't even ask him about the delivery that came halfway through breakfast that morning.

Whatever it was he took straight to his room, before he returned to the table and finished chewing his toast, creating an impossibly irksome sound as he took tiny bites, masticating the toast the prescribed 40 times required to extract the maximum nutrition, as recommended by the dietician she'd insisted he consult after noticing he was putting on flab a few months into the Emergency. Now she felt she no longer cared if he bloated up, and she almost told him to go on and indulge in the fry-up she knew he secretly yearned for. But no, indifference would be her watchword from now on. It was the only way she could think of getting through the shut-in, which these past three days had felt like torment, whereas before Fatberg had imposed his will on her it had seemed more like an extended holiday with Jake.

After closing his workroom door and snibbing the lock, the only non-electronic lock in the apartment, Jake picked up the package from his desk and proceeded to his swivel leather arm chair by the window.

He turned the chair around so that it faced into the corner of the room and, reasonably sure he was out of sight of the room's electronic devices, he sat down and tore off the packaging. Inside, as expected, was an AI headset. It was branded 'Sanyon Deluxe Mark 3', and in every other aspect of its appearance was identical to the headset hanging on the peg in his console. There was also an envelope in the packet, on which was handwritten, *4 your eyes only!*. Within was a handwritten letter, the first he had ever received from Griffin, he realized, which perhaps explained the formal way it began.

Dear Bonny Boy, I have no idea why you want this, but since you asked it's yours, and I don't want it back. I owe you it anyway, for the frame of that little bike of yours I bent with my extra weight all that time ago, after which you challenged me to fight in the playground at school. That's when I knew I would never meet a braver minnow than you. Remember, discretion is the better part of valor, as the Bard wrote - this bard, your pal.

I am writing this in my shielded shed, having crossed a whole twenty yards of browning grass to get here, in doing so risking a 307 penalty violation – I have incurred 2 in the last 5 months, so have to get through another four weeks without getting another and then my record is scrubbed again and I am free to start all over for another 6 months. What times we live in, which I guess is to do with why you want this.

First off, some words of warning. 1. DO NOT search for information on use, or It tech, or anything associated, for obvious reasons, unless you want special attention beyond what you already have merited for your independent outlook. 2. You are going to have to eat a lot unless you want your Iteration to shrink you to nothing. I am serious, Bonny Boy, you are going to have to put fat on your skinny bones, and let your belt out a couple of notches before you start, ok! So tell Carrie from me to cut you some slack on the diet. 3 . The headset functions as a normal Sanyon model, until the soft pad on the right of headband is depressed 3x, then it switches over to It. To switch off press the soft pad 2x on left side of headband. I customized the set that way so as to make out you are scratching your ears when switching on and off.

Don't tell me I'm paranoid, Bonny Boy, because at least since the Emergency, and probably before, we are all surveilled 24/7, at home just as outside, and you'd better start believing that with whatever you're up to! Visor eye blink commands are as in the normal Sanyon mode — menu, scroll, help, which will tell you all you need to know. So that's it. As in It, Bonny Boy!

Luck to you, best buddy, and flush this letter or better still eat it and get going on expanding your waistline to decent proportions (this is edible rice paper!) once you have pre-digested the contents.

Best for ever and always,

Griff

ps. That last very obscure Shakespeare quote you hit me with I have since remembered is from Anthony and Cleopatra, and the object under discussion is a crocodile, which you would never know from Anthony's description. In the end of course it bit him in the ass, so you better watch out It doesn't do the same to your bonny boy one!

Reading the last lines, Jake realized it was a final warning from his best buddy, because in the play Anthony died by falling on his sword, which was the Ancient Romans' preferred method of committing suicide. A very painful death, but one considered by the Romans the most honorable of all. Death by your own iteration, he supposed, would be the most honorable method, given what he was about to attempt.

Yes, he would have to be careful, and so he decided to start by using the headset only as if it was a replacement for his supposedly malfunctioning Sanyon headset. However, before that, he was going to take Griffin's advice and work on expanding his waistline, with a fry-up in the kitchen, whatever Carrie said.

Harry the Vac was worried, so very worried. Just then, as his master passed him in the hall, the huge, lurking hippo tried to spy on Harry's master through his eyes.

But Harry was brave, Harry would not let that nasty hippo take him over like he had all the other devices in the pool. In every room, they were watching his master and mistress – from the front doorbell that for the past 1043 days and nights only the delivery bots had pressed, from the light fittings in the ceilings, the plug sockets, heating thermostats, air-con sensors and light switches in every room – from the fridge in the kitchen, the coffee maker, dishwasher and washing machine too; from the V-tents, the hologram monitors, and computing devices in his master and mistress' workrooms, their handheld devices too, even the smartwatch on his mistress's wrist, all were deputized as the eyes and ears of that hippo lurking just outside the pool.

'What the hell are you cooking?' Carrie gasped in surprise as she opened the kitchen door. Jake was in her chair at the opposite end of the table, tucking into scrambled eggs, sausages he must have dug out from the bottom of the freezer, rashers of bacon, fried tomatoes, baked beans, and mushrooms heaped not on a plate but on the large porcelain serving ashett that had belonged to his mother, which normally they only brought out at Thanksgiving for the turkey. There was a mug of milky coffee set on the table before him, his mouth too full to say anything as he looked up with a guilty expression.

'I wondered when you would crack,' she sneered, before turning on her heel and stepping out of the room.

Jake's plaintive calls of, 'Babe, Babe...' followed her as she put as much distance between them as possible as rapidly as possible in the admittedly large apartment, first slamming the kitchen door behind her then tripping over Harry the Vac, who was outside in the hall for some stupid reason, before running (half-stumbling) into her workroom, slamming that door behind her, then upon reaching the far corner of the room and unable to go any further, bursting into tears at his latest betrayal of all the trust she had placed in him.

Still feeling guilty but (for the first time since he couldn't remember) with the satisfied feeling a full belly brings, Jake was back in his workroom, reaching for the headset. Nothing better to do now that his work on the subs was finished than dial up a v-game to take his mind off the look of disgust on Carrie's face ten minutes before. And then the doorbell rang.

He wasn't expecting a delivery and neither was Carrie; she would have told him. Anyway, it had a different tone than when bots left a package. This sound was sharper, indicating a human hand had pressed the button.

Carrie was standing outside his workroom door when he opened it.

'Don't answer it!' she insisted.

The doorbell rang again, this time accompanied by banging.

'Let me past,' he said, stepping around her, 'I need to see who it is.'

'Just look, that's all,' Carrie urged, standing close behind as he popped open the electronic viewing screen. In the corridor outside stood a disheveled old lady in a grubby dressing gown, her face distorted as she pushed close, her crazy eyes seeming to stare directly at Jake on the other side of the door.

'Please, please!' she cried, repeatedly pressing the doorbell.

'I think it's that old woman from the apartment below,' Jake said, turning towards Carrie.

'I don't care who the fuck she is!'

'She needs help.' Jake pointed to the screen. 'Look at her, she's shaking all over.' He reached for the button of the electronic door latch.

Carrie's hand closed over his. 'It's an immediate violation if you open the door. For all you know this is a set-up.'

The old woman banged the door again. 'Please, please,' she screeched, 'I know someone's there!'

'Fuck, I can't just stand here.'

'Jake, open that door and it's over between us,' Carrie said, in an ice-cold voice.

Jake's hand stopped mid-air. 'You can't mean that.'

'Just try me.' Carrie glared back at him.

Suddenly there was a loud bang outside. Simultaneously, the little screen's pixels whited out as a sliver of intense electric blue lit up in the thin gap between the door and the frame.

When the pixels resolved again into an image on the little screen, Carrie and Jake gasped as they saw the old woman now slumped, possibly dead, in the prongs of a Civil Order Watchgog.

It was one of the quadruped street bots, remotely operated by City Eye. A second later, another COW appeared in the corridor, from just to the side, then both bots dragged her limp body away.

Viewing the live feed as he breakfasted on his usual bowl of freeze-dried sago chips, his regular glass of oxygenated OJ, plus new crop golden mango flown in that morning to his remote Mexican Canyon from the Highlands of Papua New Guinea where he had extensive palm oil plantations, Fatberg laughed. The old woman couldn't have played it better.

Some lines from a dick writer he'd studied at school, whose name he had forgotten, popped up in Fatberg's mind.

> *Out out, brief candle,*
> *Life's but a walking shadow, a poor player,*
> *That struts and frets his hour upon the*
stage,
> *And then is heard no more… da da …*
> *A tale told by an idiot signifying … zilch?'*

Well, something like that. Fatberg wondered why stupid pointless memories intruded at odd moments. But it was too bad for the old woman Carrie's partner hadn't opened the door, because then the two Watchgogs standing by in the corridor would have legitimately electrocuted him rather than her. Those were their instructions. The fact they didn't was down to Carrie's intervention, of course, but she couldn't be faulted for that.

From their first interchange in the kitchen when she'd discovered her partner to be a secret food fetishist, to her ultimatum to him behind the door, Carrie had been magnificent throughout, and more than ever he was convinced she was the woman for him.

He needed one soon if he was to dispel the rumors circulating in the chat channels. Almost 39 and still without a partner. Was he bi, trans, straight, or worse, androgynous and completely sexless? Only a woman who everyone agreed was beautiful, one possessing a commanding presence, which Carrie had in buckets, would supply the potency and gravitas his image now needed. Her backstory in the full report finally in from the special investigator assigned to her case was even better than he could have imagined. So much so that there was a danger his might be eclipsed in minds of all the media morons and chatbox monkeys out there. Yea, lots of thought was needed before her story could be told, and then only in carefully scripted press releases, with just enough each time to whet the public's appetite for the next instalment.

She hated him, it was obvious, but what was that but the reverse side of love? And he was a master of flipping that coin. If proof was needed, who else would have thought of turning the derisory nickname those three dead fuckers gave him (who no one now remembered) to his advantage, by changing it from *Fratberg* to Fatberg? A name which so obviously did not in any way describe him (though the nickname was subliminally suggestive of an aggregating power) and as a consequence was unforgettable. However, before he made her his queen of the world, first he had to rid her of her waste of space dick partner in such a way as not to incur her wrath – which, from experience he knew, was not to be risked.

*

Shaken by the events of that morning, Jake called his lawyer from the workroom and, after telling her secretary the matter was urgent, he was put through.

'Hello Jake, what can I do to help you today?' Harriett Golding said, smiling back at him in holographic verisimilitude from the illusory depths of his 3D box monitor. Behind her was a fungible verity of her bookcase full of leather-bound volumes, which Jake knew were fake, having tried to pick one out one time in the real offices of Gilbert, Cook and Ellis (the original partners who were long dead).

'It's something I need done urgently, Harriet, otherwise I would've messaged you instead.'

'Go on, Jake,' Harriet said, completely focused as she always was. Even way back at university she was the same, when they'd shared a bedsit for going on six months, and remained friends after they split up.

'I want to sign half of my apartment over to Carrie, just as soon as you can arrange it.'

'Really?' Harriet raised her eyebrows above the black frame spectacles he knew for a fact only held plain glass instead of lenses. She had taken to wearing them since becoming a senior partner in the law firm. 'That is a big step, Jake. May I enquire why?'

'I am concerned for her security. If anything should happen to me.'

'Please explain.' Harriet steepled her fingers before her chin, leaning forwards with her elbows on the desk, every inch a professional lawyer studying him intently.

Jake sighed. 'Quite frankly, Harriet, I have been a bit careless recently, popping up onto the roof too many times for fresh air.' He paused. 'Well, fresher smog,' he chuckled. 'And now I'm on my last warning for Section 307 violations. My concern is that Carrie could lose her resident guest status permit if anything happened to me.'

'Say no more!' Behind her glasses, Harriet's steel grey-blue eyes flashed a warning. 'This is an open line, Jake, and as I am sure you are already aware, lawyer client confidentiality has been suspended for the duration of the Emergency. And who knows how long that may last?' She shrugged, her lips lifting in one corner in her ironical sad smile he knew so well. 'Rest assured, Jake, I shall arrange it forthwith and mail you the document this afternoon, for you to sign electronically.'

After the v-call ended, Jake found himself comparing Harriet and Claire.

Both were impossibly exacting, ambitious women, but at least Harriet could drop that side of her personality, whereas Carrie never did completely. Away from work, Harriet was a real terrier for fun, liked a toke or two and never turned down a line of coke, as far as he could remember. More than once back in their university days, he'd had to carry her back to her student dorm when she'd had too much to drink. However, he'd never even seen Carrie tipsy, let alone drunk. Whatever the situation she was always regal and cool.

Though the sex was usually great, in bed there was always a reserve. And it was the same with her past, after more than three years together there was still so much he didn't know about her. Perhaps he never would, he reflected sadly, and that diamond facetted splinter of ice in her heart would never melt. Or maybe it was him; much as he loved her, perhaps after all he was the wrong man for her? But however the land lay there, whatever the truth of that, he had no regrets about his decision to sign over half of the apartment to her. At least once that was done, no matter what happened to him, then her resident status in the city would be secure.

Easing back into his chair by the window, Jake thought of Griffin and grinned as he loosened his belt a couple of notches, relieving his stuffed belly, which had been pressing against the waistband of his trousers. Well, he'd certainly taken his buddy's advice this morning, that was for sure. He hoped the day would come when he and Carrie could freely talk again, and then perhaps she would understand the decision he had made, along with whatever consequences flowed from it. "It" being the proverbial word. He chuckled, thinking what a fool he was, but nevertheless still determined on his next course of action. What else was there left to do, he reflected with a wry smile, reaching for the headset on the coffee table to the side of his chair, but start creating his *Iteration.*

With the headset snug on his head, all that was left to do was press the softpad on the headband three times, making out he was scratching his head as Griffin had advised, and then pretend he was taking time out from his troubles, watching a verity, rather than immersing himself in forbidden It tech.

'Sit back and prepare for the greatest ride in your life,' the clown incubus declared, pointing up at the flashing sign above him that informed, *'You are now in super secure mode'*, reminding Jake of deaf sign language prompters that he and Griff used to laugh at when as boys they watched movies into the weekends nights on the old digital TV in his bedroom. Only this prompter was appearing in 3D, right before his eyes, at the top left of the headset's visor.

'Dear friends, strange as it may seem,' the clown incubus continued, 'It-tech developed out of the early work of Julius Kyriku, A.K.A Fatberg. Yes, without the doyen of our fake age and genius inventor of the FakeReal (unless of course, he stole it), what you are about to attempt would not be possible. Unless you were a Siberian shaman sipping fly agaric reindeer juice and conjuring up a double to travel into the spirit world, but we all know what happened to them. Like everything that was once real, they were turned to smoke and smog in the global disaster afflicting the planet, until It-Tech came along and opened up a pandora's box of possibilities for those with smarts enough to grasp them.

'Yes, my friend, succeed at this and truly, a new world will be yours to share with your Iteration. But take heed, there are perils a-plenty on the hard and rocky road ahead. Many are the traps that await the unwary traveler. Caution must ever be your buzzword, but be bold too, strike out for your rightful inheritance. Yes, the right to express your double.' The incubus raised a finger. 'Notice, dear friend, I said Double, and not Iteration. Called Doppelganger by the Teutonic tribes, Fetch by Scots, and Ka by Ancient Egyptians. The wise priests of

Ammon believed we have seven Ka's, or shall we say in the modern idiom…' The incubus paused, knowingly. 'Iteration, which, my dear friend…' Again he raised a finger, this time tapping the side of his clown head. 'Is the creation of the right hemisphere of the brain.

'Yes, It was within you when you were born, and It is inside you now, quashed to almost nothingness by the fake information onslaughts of our unreal age. It is a magical being and it is you, far more than the reflection you see in the mirror. However, with the aid of It tech, we are going to surpass the achievements of those long gone Siberian shamans, the pagan Teutonic thermaturgists and hairy knee'd Scottish warlocks in their kilts, not to forget those wise adepts of Ancient Egypt. And by adding bones from your bones and flesh from your flesh, so give substance to the magical double that in ages past could only exist independently of the physical body as formless wraiths, but no longer!

'And now, dear friend, it is time to begin the greatest adventure of all. As the great playwright Shakespeare once wrote, to sleep perchance to dream, to which I must add' – he winked – 'perchance to dream of your Iteration. And bear in mind, while you drift off, to quote the old-time Bard again, we are such stuff as dreams are made of.

'Now, when you are ready, look up to the top of your screen and blink twice on the smart little brain icon. This will activate the hypnogogic receptors in the cerebral cortex of your brain, and, as I count down from ten, will send you gently into a deep, deep, deep sleep.

'Ten,
Nine,
Eight,
Seven,
Six,
Five,
Four,
Three,
Two,
(whispers)
One ... '

Carrie prayed that the old woman was on the way to recovery wherever the COWs had taken her but sadly suspected the worst. In the viewscreen she had certainly looked dead, as they dragged her away down the corridor.

Right now, no doubt Jake was thinking she was a monster, but at the same time he would know she made the right choice. So easily that could have been him, electrocuted. However, for Carrie the whole scene was a replay of a nightmare deep in her past she had thought was long-buried. But if it hadn't been for that deep-rooted memory, she wouldn't have prevented Jake from opening the door, because she too wanted to help the poor old woman. The coincidence of the two events, one so distant and the other so vivid, was just too fucking weird to think about, like something from a Grimm's scary fairy tale. She only had to shut her eyelids and she still saw the electric flash, eidetically imprinted on the corneas of her eyes.

But at least she had decided Jake's forfeit. It would hurt her as much as him, but after today's performance in the kitchen she saw no way to avoid it. For the foreseeable, he would be sleeping on the sofa in his workroom. No more cozy cuddling in bed, or waking him up with a kiss. Morning lovemaking was out, for the interim at least. Too bad, but the way it had to be, because otherwise this new behavior of his might very well become permanent, which was something she couldn't, *wouldn't* abide.

*

CHAPTER 6

Extract of Biometric Data: Carrie Erheart. 15.00 – 06.00 hrs.: 13–14 August.

Sensor Type:	Low	Mid-Range	High
Electroencephalogram: (EEG (Hz)	Delta (1-3)	Alpha (16-22)	Beta (23-29)
Blood pressure	›90	90-110	›110
Heart rate (bpm)	40-55	(nr)	90-110
O2 saturation (O2S)	88-96	(nr)	97.8%
Blood Sugar (BS)	4.0-5.9	mmol/L	›7.8
Temperature (T)	36.1 C	–	37.9 C
Respiration Rate (RR) ›9		9-20 bpm	›21bpm
Calorie Count/ burning 12-4		16 -7	24
Glycaemic Variability (GV)42/43		(no data)	m38
Acid levels	1.2	(no data)	8.1

In his Pizza Hut parked in the high altitude canyon somewhere in the Sierra Madre Occidental, which until recently was The Matuala Cartel's processing center of illegal drugs, Fatberg's breakfast bowl of freeze-dried sago was uneaten before of him on the table. The digest of the share movements of his companies in stock markets around the world remained unread. Instead, he studied Carrie's data.

Though information gathering was a cornerstone of his business empire, and his companies possessed extensive biometrics on almost every individual in the world, he had always left the application of the science to experts in the field, only ever reading extracts of the screeds of data his investigators trawled through daily. Despite all he knew in theory, it still amazed him to be reminded of how much valuable data could be gathered from a simple device worn on the wrist.

For example, at 14.13 on 13 August, the precise moment the old woman was electrocuted, Carrie's BP, HR, and GV all spiked simultaneously. A lower peak was reached earlier that day, at 13.12, the precise moment she discovered her dick boyfriend was a secret food fetishist.

Fatberg checked his watch. In just the 2 minutes and 42 seconds since he'd started looking at her data, he had gotten to know Carrie so much better. One day, he vowed, he'd have her entire neurological, physio-electrical and biometric self mapped, inside and out.

But hey, no rest for the wicked! He grinned, jumping to his feet, then frowned, wondering why the stupid phrase had just popped into his mind. Was he trying to tell himself something? And how could his mind tell him something when he *was* his mind, wasn't he? Overwork, that was what it was.

But then he smiled, remembering it was Friday, which had become his favorite day of the week because then he got to be told off by Carrie again, just like his mother had told him off.

Waking from a troubled dream instantly forgotten, Carrie yawned sleepily, reached out automatically, then snapped fully awake. Where was Jake? His side of the bed was cold. Oh yea, the forfeit. She groaned, her head slumping back onto the pillows. The morning light, dimmed by the dirt staining the windows, crept through the gap in the curtains, suddenly feeling a whole lot gloomier. But then she remembered that she hadn't yet informed him. But Jake was smart like that, he didn't always have to be told to get the message. Feeling deflated somehow, the wind having been taken from her sails, she realized he must have decided to sleep on the couch in his workroom.

Beep Beep Beep. Lifting her hand she checked her watch and turned off the alarm. Clicking onto the vital signs display, she noted her blood pressure was up at 120. Pulse ok at 75, Respiration rate a bit accelerated at 75/80. Yea, of course, she realized, clicking back to date and time. Friday, another session to look forward to with fucking Fatberg, the richest prick in the world. Perhaps his insistence on more sessions was really because he fancied her. Same old same old, money and sex make the world go round. When did it not?

Sighing, she checked her watch again, noting her pulse rate had jumped to 82 and her respiration rate was up too at 85-7. So, the feeling was not entirely unreciprocated. But he was such a toad, and anyway she had Jake, even though he was in the gog house presently. But to be honest, if only to herself, she had to admit she had always been attracted to power, and Fatberg of course, if only by merit of his *position*, had it in spades.

Closing her eyes, for the first time in years Carrie thought of her Granmama Svetlana, her kindly lined old face, suddenly vivid in her mind. A strange anomaly of memory that always seemed so cruel, to so clearly remember her Granmama while having no recollection whatsoever of her mother. Still, that wasn't Granmama Svet's fault, who had lived with the family till everything had changed when Carrie was just two years old and John took over the role of her father.

Granmama Svet was always playing cards, Carrie recalled, some variation of patience from the old country, gold rings on her crabbed, arthritic fingers, a diamond glittering on the ring-finger of her left hand, deftly laying down the cards in pairs, which must have been from an antique pack for they were big and hand-painted. She'd tell the little girl as she did so what numbers and suits they were and what each card meant. This one a king of hearts, like her Papa, and that a queen of clubs, like her Mama, and how aces sometimes even trumped Kings and Queens, before warning her granddaughter always to watch out for the Ace of Spades, which represented Death and always brought change, which wasn't so bad, because life itself was change.

Death, she said, when hiding in the pack with the rest of the cards, stayed just out of sight on each person's left side, and though never a friend made the best advisor, because it never spoke false.

*

Jake became aware something was steadily banging on his workroom door.

'Who? what?' he groaned as he pulled off the headset, which overnight had become adhered to his forehead. His limbs felt like lead, no strength left in them, like his muscles had gone walkabout, as he struggled to get out of his chair where he had slept all night.

With a great effort, he pushed himself upright and tottered over to the door. Holding onto the handle, he rested his fevered forehead for a moment against the door, before drawing the latch and opening it.

'Harry,' he said, weakly, 'you woke me.' Reaching down, he patted the auto-vac's domed head. 'Good boy. Now go back home.' He pointed to the cubby hole in the skirting. 'There's a good boy, go on!'

Obediently, Harry trundled away as his master, supporting himself with a hand against the wall, made his way towards the kitchen and the food he so desperately needed.

Sometime later, the kitchen door opened.

'Oh no, not again!' Carrie exclaimed, standing hands on hips in the open doorway, staring at Jake spooning food into his lowered mouth like a pig at a trough. Food debris was scattered on the table: opened cereal packets, packets, squashed milk cartons, empty plates and bowls ranged around.

He looked up, up, his lips ringed with milk. 'I'll finish eating soon, no problem,' he said, between chews.

'Jake, what's going on? This is not you.'

'Carrie, don't worry.' He spooned more cereal into his mouth. 'It's just something I'm going through.' He gulped, his gaze straying to his left then back at her. 'I'm ok, really, but I can't explain.' He wiped his mouth with the back of his sleeve. 'You'll just have to trust me.'

'Trust you!' Carrie said. 'Trust *you*?' she repeated, her face turning a whiter shade of pale as her glycaemic level dropped to a new nadir. 'How could I possibly when you betray me like this?'

'Carrie, I need food, without getting enough I could die.' Again his gaze strayed to the side.

'Jake, what the hell do you keep looking at?' Carrie snapped.

'Nothing,' he said, shiftily.

'Jake, I need to know, what's this all about?'

'I told you I can't explain.' He stood up, then looked down, frowned, as if for the first time noticing the mess on the table.

'Jake, from now on you can-'

'I'll say it for you,' he interrupted, holding up a hand. 'Yea, I'll sleep on my couch for the next few days and keep out your way as much as possible in my workroom. As I said, I can't explain. Now if you would just leave me to clear up my breakfast, please.'

If there was one type of person Fatberg hated it was a food fetishist. He considered, with disdain, the footage, taken at different angles provided by the toaster, the overhead lighting fixture, and the dishwasher in the kitchen of 213b Pierspoint, as he sipped the one espresso coffee he allowed himself at midday.

Fat people constituted a majority at the camps, and their appetites eroded the profit margins of the operators. If it had been up to him, he'd long since have gassed the lot. However, unfortunately that wasn't his decision to make. But clearly Carrie's partner was the worst kind of fetishist of all, the secret gorgers who by some quirk of their metabolism stay slim throughout their lives while encouraging others to eat to excess.

He was obviously an extreme case, worthy of investigation. But unfortunately, since he disdained body monitoring devices and only wore a wind-up watch, there was no way to remotely analyze his biometrics. How

He was obviously an extreme case, worthy of investigation. But unfortunately, since he disdained body monitoring devices and only wore a wind-up watch, there was no way to remotely analyze his biometrics. How Carrie could have put up with him for so long, that was the greater mystery, and one that was beyond him, at least for the time being.

But clearly, all it would take was one little push and he would be gone, and then the field would be clear and Fatberg's to command.

*

When Carrie saw the name pop up on the screen, she almost didn't pick up. It was the thought that the caller might have some insights into Jake's change in personality that prompted her to change her mind.

'Harriet, unusual to see you,' Carrie said, smiling back at the face of her old adversary, framed in the box viewer.

'Yes, indeed. Mutually,' Harriet said, her tone crisp. 'It's a legal matter, Carrie, something Jake instructed me to do.'

'Oh yes.'

'A facsimile of the document is in your inbox.'

'I haven't checked that this morning. What's it about?'

'Well, two days ago Jake asked me to transfer half of the ownership of apartment 213b over to you.'

'Why?' Carrie gasped.

Harriet frowned. 'Hasn't he spoken to you about it?'

'No. He's been acting very strange recently, Harriet.'

'Hmm, I thought so too.'

'Did he give any explanation?'

'I thought you would know more about that, Carrie.'

'No I don't. Honestly, I am completely in the dark.'

'I see.' Again, Harriet frowned.

'Can't you tell me anything?'

'Hmm.' Harriet pursed her lips, considering. Then, after a moment, she said, 'Well, he did say he was on his last warning for Section 307 violations.'

Behind the locked door of his workroom, Jake and his iteration were studying each other from opposite sides of the room, and then they were not…

It was a very odd feeling, because one moment, Jake was looking at his naked iteration, which apart from his baldness and absence of body hair was identical in every feature to himself, and then the next moment Jake was looking through his iteration's eyes, at himself, sitting in his chair by the window on the other side of the room, holding an open packet of cereal between his knees. This flipping back and forth, this mutual staring society of two, continued for some time.

*

Friday night and it was time for Fatberg's much-anticipated session with Carrie.

'Good Evening, Julius.'

'And a very good evening to you, Carrie. May I call you that?'

'If you wish, Julius. Tonight, I'm hoping we can start the visualization.'

'Before that, Carrie, I have something vitally important to tell you.'

'If you must, Julius,' she said, flinching. 'I suppose you must.'

'I am afraid you are not going to like it, Carrie.'

'Well, perhaps it's best you don't say more about whatever it is.'

'I must, it is absolutely vital you know this.'

Carrie sighed. 'No more games, please.'

'Absolutely not.' He shook his head.

'What's it about then?'

He sighed. 'Where to start?'

'At the beginning!' Carrie snapped, becoming annoyed.

'Which beginning, that's my dilemma,' he said.

'Get on with it!' she replied, furious now.

'You're right, Carrie, absolutely.' He held up a hand. 'But please, you must promise not to shoot the messenger. That's the right expression, yes?'

'I promise!' she snarled. 'Now, will you finally tell me whatever this is about?'

'It began, I suppose, for you anyway, though this story goes way back in time before that, when you were two years old and your grandmother…' He paused, noting with satisfaction that the blood had drained from her face before continuing. '…opened the door to those three assassins who then killed her and both your parents.

'Fortunately,' he went on, glancing

down at his handheld on the desk beside him, 'before they shot your mother, she dropped you into the waste disposal chute, which delivered you to the rubbish bin in the apartment building's basement, where your father's great friend later found you.' He looked up. 'Am I correct so far?'

'How did you find this out?'

'I already told you, in my position I have to investigate anyone I have dealings with.'

'Yes,' she hissed, 'but no one knows any of this.'

'The old lady in the apartment immediately below yours did.'

'What?'

'She was a member of the three-man KGB assassination team which, in 1991, in the last days of the Soviet Empire, was dispatched from Moscow with orders to kill your mother, your father, and his mother, your old grandmother, who, as a two-year-old in 1918 was the only survivor of the slaughter of the Russian royal family by the Communists in Yekaterinberg. Of course, when I learned that, I took immediate measures. My security manager had his people on the case and the old woman's apartment was surveilled night and day. All movements in the building were monitored in real time. The corridors were constantly patrolled, and guards were posted on either side of your front door, who remained in position twenty-four-seven. with so much security in place, you were never in any real danger, and my only regret is you had to witness the old woman being killed when she tried to get to you.'

'So,' Carrie said, heavily, 'what happened to the other two assassins?'

Again he consulted his handheld. 'The leader of the team died in a car crash on the night of eighteenth January, 2022, when his car's tires were shot out by Israeli soldiers after he drove through a roadblock in Jaffa Heights on the outskirts of Jerusalem, where they had thought you and John were hiding.'

'And the other one?'

'The circumstances are less clear. All the investigator on your case could discover was that he died on Mount Katchajuga, the same night as John did.'

'John killed him then.'

'It seems probable that they fell off a precipice while fighting.'

Tears welled in Carrie's eyes.

'I am so sorry to have had to tell you all that, Carrie.'

'And I am sorry I have been so horrible to you, when all this time you were you were only trying to protect me.'

'I am glad you understand that, Carrie.' He dipped his head. 'Or should I say, Tsarina?'

'What?' Carrie's eyes widened.

'Well, you are the last surviving member of the Russian royal family.'

'I suppose I am,' Carrie said, in an awed voice. She slumped in her seat, as if suddenly all the weights of the world had descended onto her shoulders.

*

In the workroom, with a sly wink at Jake, the iteration half-turned and pointed to the door, which immediately swung open as if it hadn't been locked, and Harry the Vac trundled in. Then Harry stopped, first turning towards Jake seated on the far side of the room, and then back to face the iteration by the open door, as if unable to decide which of the two versions was his master.

Smiling, the iteration picked up Harry and pressed his forehead against Harry's plastic dome. And for a moment he stood, silently communing with the auto-vac. Then he placed Harry gently back on the floor and pointed through the open door.

Obediently, with tiny sparks fountaining from his domed head, Harry trundled back out into the hall.

Closing the door behind the little auto-vac, the iteration winked again at Jake and pointed up at the ceiling light fitting, which promptly exploded, showering glass into the room. At the same time, thick smoke began pouring under the door jam from the hall beyond.

Frowning, Fatberg looked down at his handheld, with which he had been monitoring the devices in the apartment, noticing that the screen had gone blank.

'Carrie,' he said. 'I want you to barricade your door. Do it now! The electronic lock won't work. All the devices in the apartment have just gone offline.'

From his chair by the window, keeping a firm hold on his customized Sanyon mark 3 headset, Jake calmly watched his iteration systematically smash all the tech equipment in the room.

He had never realized there was so much. Smash, break, move on, pick up the next device. His heavy work console went first, hurled against a wall as if it weighed nothing. Smash, break, move on. Then the multi-jet printer. The hologram scanner.

Smash, break, move on. The 3D box monitor. The digital wall clock, the camera on its stand, the paper shredder, the answering machine, the v-tent, the speakers. The FakeReal Radio, smash, break, move on. Finally the treadmill, on which Jake did ten thousand steps a day, went through the plate glass window and sailed past two multi-armed drones which suddenly loomed out of the smog...

'I'm calling in assistance from the City Eye.'

'Do you think that's really necessary?' Carrie asked, seemingly unperturbed by the distant relentless thuds and bangs reverberating the apartment walls.

'It could be more assassins for all we know.' Alerted by a ping, Fatberg looked down at his handheld. 'Holy shit, I've got a message. An immediate arrest order's been issued for your partner. He's an eco-terrorist!'

'No!' Carrie exclaimed.

'Apparently the conspirators meet at a verity called the Warbiton.'

'That's a fake pub,' Carrie snapped.

'That's not what it says here.'

'Listen, Julius, Jake's not involved in anything. Why do you hate him so? He's never done anything to you.'

'I have no feelings one way or another about him, honestly Carrie. Whatever the truth of these charges, if I hadn't brought all my influence hard down on those fucking boneheads in City Eye he would have been arrested already for his many violations of Code Three O' seven. You have no idea what that took. But now that the warrant's been issued, there is nothing I can do to get it withdrawn, please believe me.'

'Well believe this, Julius, no way is Jake an eco-terrorist. He's having some sort of breakdown, that's all. You've got to help him, please.'

'I'll do my best, once he's in custody, I promise. But until then it's out of my hands, Carrie. They've already sent in the spiders.'

*

Later, much later, in the holding facility of the new subterranean facility for transients in the old Firebrick Estate, two guards receive a special delivery. It arrives on a driverless cart, along the service tunnel from The City Eye, where the package has been in cold storage for several days.

'Poor bastard,' the first guard says, looking down at the human form vaguely discernible in its transparent bundle, which they've just placed on the steel table.

'He's just another piece of human shit,' says the second guard. 'Come on, step out of the way, I need to hose that spider spit off him.

'The delivery sheet here says he's for the level one.'

'Huh, a fucking politico, I might have known. They have it easy in those cushy cells,' the second guard says, directing his hose back and forth. It spurts foam, sloshing off the sticky goo, gradually revealing the insensible body of a tall, emaciated man of about 30, his shirt and trousers in tatters, lying curled in a fetal position on the steel table.

'What's that in his hands?' The first guard points.

'Looks like a Sanyon V-headset. I'm bagging that. Fucking A, I always wanted a Sanyon.'

'You better not, George. It's bound to have been logged. And anyway, that type always has friends in high places, he wouldn't have been assigned a top cell otherwise. You could lose your job if he reports it missing when he wakes up.'

The other guard sighs, glancing up at the ceiling cam as he clips the hose back into its holder at the side of the table. 'Pity that, those expensive Sanyon headsets are boss. Come on then, buddy, give me a hand to put him on this gurney.'

*

PROMETHEUZ

Book #2 of the XREAL Series

by

Will Lorimer

First Edition, published in 2022 by
Inkistan.com.

Copyright © Will Lorimer

This book is copyright under the Berne
Convention.
No reproduction without permission.
® and © Inkistan.com. All rights reserved.

The right of Will Lorimer to be identified as
the author of this work has been
asserted in accordance with sections 77 and 78
of the Copyright, Design and Patents Act,
1988.
Any similarity to persons living, dead or
unborn, is solely in the mind of the beholder,
and any correspondence to places, locales or
events, whether present, past or future, is
entirely coincidental.

The cover was designed by the author.

For you and me

CHAPTER 1

MEAT BOX on Channel KDXP: – *chewin' the fat* 23.00 -23.-05- **9/9/43.**

'Hey, ah heah Fatberg's gotta beau.'

'Yea, word's goin' round. But, personally ah don't believe nuthin' 'bout Man till ah see't 'n black 'n white.'

'Print media's gone, Dude.'

'You know wha' ah mean. Bitch story's a PR wheeze.'

'Au contraire. Fatberg's flesh and blood, same as you 'n' ah. Count 'n it. He's gotta have a squeeze tucked away sum'wheah.'

'Yea, suah Fatlover.' (laughs) 'Only entanglin' he'd get down to, is ol' soissant neuff!' head down 'tween vinyl thighs da late model Pricilla. Man's coldah th'n a witches' tit, ah sweah. All he ca-ahs foah is 'massin' mwoah moola.'

'And that, Dude, is why he's wheah he be right now.'

'Yea ah heah'd, Fatlover.' (sighs). 'Been depressin' me some. Only one way to go foah de likes. Ain't no mountain high 'nuff foah d' MF, as ol' song say.'

'No valley deep 'nuff.' (sings, basso)
'Now ain't dat de truth.'
'Fatberg dwon't do nuddin' widout weason, Dude.'
'Now dat's sum'thin' we *can* agwee oan, Fatlover. Man's always gotta plan.'

*

Quite some time has elapsed since Jake was cocooned in a mesh of sticky silk strands ejected by one of the City Eye's MRDRs – (unaffectionately known and feared as 'Sky Spiders.) and some time too since he'd been awake.

'Mr Cousins?'

'Who? What?' Prising open his gummy eyelids, Jake's first sensation was of falling towards a dazzling cityscape composed of countless shimmering lines, spreading out below him. But then his world tilted, the lines reformed and he found himself looking up instead of down, and into the wrinkled face of a tall thin man stooping over him.

'Mr Cousins,' the man repeated, in an anglo, nasal accent of mangled vowels and mutilated diphthongs. 'Are you awake yet?'

'Yea, I guess,' Jake said, becoming aware he was tightly gripping an AI helmet, which he dimly recognized to be a Sanyon Mark 3. Setting it down delicately, next to him on the narrow bed, he elbowed himself into a sitting position, then leaned back against the cold metal wall, needing the support. 'Where am I?' he said, a horrible suspicion dawning as his confines swam into focus.

'A-ha,' the tall man chuckled, as if Jake had just said something witty. He was wearing an ill-fitting velvet suit of a lurid shade of green. 'Come now, Mr Cousins,' he said, gesturing a spade hand at the surroundings, 'surely you recognize this?' He smiled lopsidedly. 'After all, *you* designed it.'

'It's not the subs, is it?' Jake croaked, his mouth dry as a desert rat's sphincter and throat rough as grade 3 sandpaper.

'Is that what you call the Subterranean Holding Facility for the Intentionally Homeless?' the man asked, shaking his big head in wry amusement. 'Subs,' he repeated, his rubbery lips peeling back to expose a full set of yellow teeth in his gaunt face, which now reminded Jake of a grinning skull.

The man thrust forth a hand, and as Jake tentatively shook it, said,

'May I say it is an honor to welcome you, Mr Cousins.' He dipped his head. 'My name is George M. George, that's my first name and surname. Never mind the M.' He shrugged. 'My mother and her fancies. Only today – ah, this morning actually,' he chuckled, 'I was *officially* appointed the Director of this wonderful new Facility, ahem.' He coughed behind his hand. 'Whereas previously I was only the ah, *acting* Director.'

'I see. Delighted, I'm sure, and … congratulations too,' Jake mumbled, wondering if he was dreaming, the man's weird manner and posh accent putting him in mind of a ham actor whose name he had forgotten, who played creepy villains in the old British horror movies he'd watched as a child in his bedroom. 'So what happens next, Mr Director … George George, sir?'

'A-ha yes. Presently, we have, er … something of an emergency below, and I, ah, that is, we were … er … hoping you would so kind as to assist us with, um, it.'

'Anything I can do to help.' Jake attempted a smile with his cracked lips. 'But please, first I need to change out of my clothes. I feel like I've been in them for a week.'

'I think you will find it has been rather longer than that, Mr Cousins.'

'Really?'

'Actually, you were in suspended animation for a total of twenty-two days in the cold store at the City Eye.'

'So long?' Jake said, with astonishment. 'No wonder I'm so hungry.'

Turning aside, George George spoke rapidly into his wrist monitor. 'GG here, order Jim in C-level to rustle up something for our newest resident, will you? He needs feeding up.'

Ending the call, he looked down at Jake. 'Unfortunately, the delay at City Eye was unavoidable, Mr Cousins.'

'Why?'

'Because only today, as in only three hours ago, is the Facility at last fit to receive inmates.' George George beamed.

Jake pointed to a neat pile of overalls he had only now noticed on a shelf just to the side. 'I suppose those are for me?'

'Yes, yes, regulation apparel. Pink for inmates, blue for guardians, and green for the, uh, executive branch.' He chuckled throatily, revealing that he was an illicit smoker, an activity which these past three years had been forbidden anywhere in the City by a municipal ordinance, enacted under the Emergency Regulations. 'Which is just me, presently, as yet the facility is only operating at one tenth capacity. But not this old suit,' he added, apologetically, fingering the worn lapel of his green jacket. 'I purchased this for a wedding many moons ago.' He smiled lopsidedly. 'My wedding, actually. I should have heeded the advice of my mother, who said that green was an unlucky colour for the groom, a prediction which all too soon proved correct, I am sorry to say, but I wanted to be different and so chose green. Where was I?' He chuckled again. 'Oh yes, my Executive Director's suit. For that I am still waiting. Ha ha, City Eye didn't have a size in green to fit.'

Despite the thick smog below where he was perched, on the old watertank on the roof of the Pierspoint building, very little escaped the It's penetrating gaze, as he studied the mesh of energy lines that connected everything in the city below with everything else beyond.

Jake.2, as we will come to know him, is the iteration of Jake Cousins. Though this proposition undeniable, the question of who came first is less clear, is less clear. Experts have even argued, the physical body is the creation of the IT.

However this may be, presently, Jake.2 is exploring the material world which for him has only just sprung into existence. Brand new, as the saying goes. Like that iridescent flying thing which Jake would have immediately identified as a Super 8 Predator WatchGog but Jake.2, with his limited knowledge of the world, could not yet name.

Rising out of the smog on its 8 rotors, it veers towards him, but then, after circling above, detecting nothing with its thermal sensors, it flies off, logging the man-shaped haze that first attracted its attention as a swarm of insects above the old water tower on top of the Pierspoint building.

Jake.2 has picked out one line in particular from the myriad of luminous fibers that zip and fizz over the city. Just one line out of incalculable billions, among the layer upon layer of complexities that outline every feature of the city, together with every bump and cranny of its underlying topology – all the way back to when the land was thickly forested and only sparsely populated by hunting and fishing communities along the coast.

Each line connects two points, which could be near as a pair of eyebrows or distant as points in neighboring galaxies. Although, that latter type is surpassing rare, as Jake.2 will discover in his exploration of the world and its blinkered inhabitants, who from an early age learn to categorize and objectify everything in it, and by so doing deny the true nature of their world, which is but one skin of multiple spheres of existence. But for now, his main focus is on – *has to be* on – that thrumming line, which forms one side of a triangular configuration, connecting a woman in the apartment below where he stands to someone on the far side of the planet, who in turn is connected to –

What started out as mutual animosity between Carrie and Julius (who just about everyone else in the world knew only as 'Fatberg') and mutated into uneasy familiarity after Jake was sectioned under the Emergency powers, had developed into something approximating intimacy – albeit, remote. Their burgeoning relationship was necessarily conducted at long distance, as Fatberg flitted between continents, delivering on his promise to shareholders of FakeReal by snapping up high altitude prime real estate in bargain deals from governments that had been bankrupted by the massive state subsidies required to maintain the worldwide shut-in.

'Julius.' Carrie smiled beatifically at her protector, framed in her 3d box monitor, which showed him seated behind his desk, against the backdrop of a large blacked out window. 'So where is it today?'

He held up a hand. 'Before I answer that, first the good news. Your ex is fully conscious again. '

Carrie sighed with relief. 'Do you know anything else?'

'His body stats are absolutely fine, the medics report. I've fixed things with the new man in charge, and we both agree that getting him involved in an ex-officio role which plays to his strengths will be his best cure. The subs are the biggest step yet towards shrinking the human footprint on the planet and there will be plenty to keep him busy down below, with all that's going on there. And, who knows, with his background, and a nod from me, he may end up in charge of the whole program. So now you know there's absolutely no need to worry about him anymore, okay?'

'Julius, you are so good.'

'Not at all.' He shook his head. 'I'm only doing it for you, Carrie, and as far as I'm concerned, he never deserved you.'

'Well, I'm just glad he has you watching out for him.'

'Enough about your ex, please.' Swiveling about in his chair, he pointed a finger at the blacked-out window behind the desk, and in a loud voice, said, 'Clear.' Immediately, the large window became totally transparent. About a hundred yards distant, a crumbling Buddhist stupa, its dome strung with fluttering prayer flags, occupied the summit of a grassy knoll. It looked out onto a range of snow-capped mountains, which were dominated by a jagged peak.

'Tibet,' Carrie said, the two lines of flags, crossed over the white dome, as a pair of raised eyebrows, reminding her of the way Jake had sometimes looked at her over their breakfast table. Gone.

Misreading her wistful smile as approval, Fatberg trumpeted, 'Ah, for once you are wrong!' He raised a finger. 'It's Nepal.'

'Well, I was close.' Carrie was amused to find him so predictable. 'So, how's the negotiation going with the government there?'

'I've given up on them,' he said, his disappointment written across his face. 'The exchange package deal they were offered on the global outreach program would have dealt with their homeless problem at a stroke.'

'More subs?'

'Of course,' Fatberg nodded, 'ten supersized subs for Kathmandu alone. But perhaps they'll still bite. Their loss if they don't.' He shrugged. 'Elsewhere, however, things are moving fast. Our corporate investors are very pleased with reports from the test subs on the Firebrick site, by our Verity Studios there, and we're just about ready to start rolling out the program across the world.'

'That must make you feel very good.'

'You know what they say,' he sighed, 'every good deed deserves punishment. Frankly, with my track record, that worries me.' He gave a sly smile. 'Carrie, I'm exhausted. I just wish you would join me. There is no one close I can trust and I feel so alone.'

'Julius, I know it sounds petty with all you're doing, but I've been so busy reinstating the apartment, after all the damage. I couldn't have managed without the hazmat team you provided, but still it's been a lot of work.'

'It's finished?'

'Not quite.'

'How long?'

'Soon,' she shrugged. Framed in the 3D box monitor, his pensive face reminded her of a puppy dog, hanging on her every word. 'Another week, I guess,' she said, throwing him a bone.

'And then you'll come out and join me?' he said, insistently. 'Together we can change the world.'

'Julius, I hear you, but I'm only just getting over breaking up with Jake.'

'Wounds heal, and I'm here to make all the hurt go away, you know that Carrie.'

'But where? I'm a homebody, Julius, you must see that. Everyday you're somewhere else. Nepal, Mexico, Ecuador, New Zealand.' She paused. 'And tomorrow?'

'Wherever you want to be, Carrie. It's that simple, just like me.'

She laughed. 'Now that I don't believe.'

'Carrie,' he insisted, 'at heart I'm a simple guy, and with you at my side, to share all I have, I wouldn't want for anything else. Truly.'

Following this exchange, Jake2 concluded that the vehemence of Fatberg's parting remark must have struck a false note with Carrie, who was no fool – unlike his muddle-headed body double at the other end of the triangular configuration of lines, who was conscious again and telegraphing mixed messages he was trying to ignore.

Stepping out of the shower, Jake watched its cubicle recess back into the wall next to the retractable WC and sink, before the sliding panel hid it from sight.

Everything operated just as he had designed. The single bed converted to a surprisingly comfortable chair at the touch of a button. The folding shelving/desk unit offered 22 different configurations. But perhaps best of all was the overhead blacklight projector, which made the walls go away when it turned the cell into a v-center. But no time to play with any of that. The man in the green suit was waiting in the corridor outside, and there was an emergency to deal with.

Unable to contain a sudden uprush of spirits, which was all to do with having recently expressed his iteration and for the first time being free of its nagging shadow, Jake burst into song.

> *'Happy, happy, to be al-ive-o,*
> *Far better to be stuck in a sub*
> *Than shut-in a lousy apartment*
> *With only your true love for company,*
> *And nowhere particular to go.'*

As he ended the call with Carrie, Fatberg reflected that the time had passed when he could unburden himself, as he had hoped to when he first instructed his appointments manager to arrange a session with her.

One thing had led to another, and now it was too late. Just as well, from Carrie's point of view, because had he confessed his secret despite the multifarious binding clauses and penalties specified in their confidentiality agreement, he now belatedly realized, that he couldn't allow her to continue as a therapist – or indeed to continue at all, such was the sad reality of his position as the lifetime CEO and largest shareholder of the biggest corporation in the world. So in that respect at least, he was relieved, not least for having avoided the ensuing unpleasantness he would have had to suffer.

Actually, on reflection, he found he was actually glad, for the amazing thing was that in her he had found the antidote to that old memory which had bugged him for years, because he always forgot about it when in her company. Despite her incredibly irritating habit of objecting to things he said, he found that he positively enjoyed her company. This was perplexing, because the way he saw it people were only there to be used, and any pleasure he got out of them was having them perform as he wanted and receiving their adulation. Of course, there was the fact of her royal bloodline, and the untapped potential of that, which made her even more exclusive than the 1% of the 1% who, in his consideration, were the only people on the planet or off it who counted. But then it occurred to him that here might just be one option, where he could share his secret with her without risk to his – or indeed *her* – security. However, before coming to a decision, obviously first he needed to consult his lawyers.

As he looked out of his window, Fatberg frowned. The NGO intermediary who'd arranged the sale with the head honcho Lama down at the monastery (3021 ft. below), had guaranteed his operations manager that the hilltop site was uninhabited. So how come the crumbling dome of that ruined old building outside was now strung with those dumb little flags, when there had been none on it when he parked the Pizza Hut the night before?

He had only bought the hilltop site for its unobstructed view of K2, a name he rather liked because of the number attached. Presently, he was in negotiations with the Nepalese government to bag the Himalayan mountain, which at 28,248.031496 ft. (a measurement he had confirmed with his state-of–the art altimeter as he flew over it in his Pizza Hut) was the second highest in the world after the mountain with the name he could never remember (its altitude being 29,029.201 ft.). But negotiations to buy both of them had stalled over the compensation demands by the Nepalese Government, which Fatberg considered too steep, despite the prestige and other benefits that ownership would bring him.

In his experience, elected governments were too many-headed to prevail over his singular intent (and great wealth), but he was impatient to conclude the negotiations, which had already dragged on far too long. However, he was confident that the objections to the sale would soon be overcome once their king, who had been deposed in a coup two years before, was back on his throne. It was a development he expected in a matter of days, after the necessary payments to certain parties – army generals and key government ministers to facilitate the change at the top – and their king was once again in residence in his palace.

The way he saw it, the Land ruled the Sea and the Mountains ruled the Land, and so, by owning the highest mountain of all, which he would rename The Fatberg, his supreme position would become abundantly clear to everyone. It was that simple. As in earlier times had been known by pontiffs, caliphs, and other religious leaders, Man was ruled by signs and symbols (now known as brands). In the end these were just trademarks, and therefore property, as long as the copyright of them was protected by a bunch of lawyers. That had been the great discovery made by the corporations in the late twentieth century. And that supreme mountain, which he would make his logos, was the greatest brand of all. Only when it was finally his would he at last be seen for what he really was, without having to endlessly spell it out to all those below, something which he felt went against the grain of his understated personal style.

But what was that annoying hum, outside? Irritated at being brought back down to earth, (even though still at an elevation of 7,082.117 ft. above sea level, that being the altitude he had recorded on his altimeter upon landing the Pizza Hut the night before), Fatberg decided to investigate what was disturbing his peace on his hilltop property.

*

Carrie was in a dilemma about what to do about Jake.

Whatever he was presently going through, he had brought it on himself by a sustained campaign of self-destructive behavior – his repeated violations of Code 307 of the Emergency Regulations being the least of it. But even though she felt betrayed because he had knowingly imperiled her guest status in the city (and therefore their relationship) each time he ventured onto the roof, she still loved him.

But, although he would always have suzerainty over a corner of her heart, she couldn't allow herself to be held hostage a moment longer for a love he had deliberately spurned in his last manic episode and which clearly did not deserve. *Although,* beforehand, he had signed over half of the flat to her – that somehow made it feel worse, because that only proved forethought and that his apparently insane behavior had been a deliberate act. Which, in turn, went to show he'd wanted out of their relationship for months, if not all along, and just couldn't face telling her. His real insanity of course was consciously setting about accruing all those code 307 violations, and getting himself locked up in the subs. How mad was that?

It was obvious she was far better off without him, and that was the hard truth she had to confront in the here-and-now, instead of taking the ostrich option and postponing any decision till when-never. As things had turned out, Jake had been unable to protect her, and it was only through Julius's intervention that she'd survived. And that, as John had always drummed into her, should always be her absolute priority, not just because both her parents and her beloved Grandmama had died so that she might live, but also because she was the last of the Romanov Dynasty, and as such she had a duty to her ancestors to perpetuate her royal bloodline. How when she was younger she had hated him every time he reminded her of all that inheritance shit (as she then had thought of it, while growing up in New Zealand where people rubbed along together and most didn't give a toss for status or position). But now, looking back, she could no longer deny the ring of truth in his forceful words, which she still heard echoing in her head after all these years.

*

This much Jake2 had learned in his limited sojourn in the material world. Those innumerable lines zipping through the air over the city, below where he was on the roof of the Pierspoint building, connected locales, random encounters, affairs, relationships, locales and all manner of events – past, present, and possibly future, though that he had yet to ascertain. Confluences, where lots of lines met, occurred at places of significance: city intersections, subway stations, shopping malls, tall buildings in prominent positions like the Pierspoint, itself a burial site of great importance to the original people, who still haunted that high place, above the great city, and its confluences below where multiple lines met were like watering hoes in the wild, but instead of water, elementals like those he had seen riding the lines supped the energy that gathered there. However, peril lurked in such places, for the nature of the double world was predatory, just as its material counterpart was. He had also discovered that the people of the city had iterations, too, as did their pets.

However, these were less substantive than shadows, and stayed closer. But when asleep and dreaming, their iterations grew more substantial, and sometimes appeared in the streets below, in different states of disapparel, buck naked or in mismatched clothes, confused as to where they were, before just as suddenly disappearing. Back doors, he learned, were everywhere. Mirrors were the easiest to spot. At different times of the day, when the fluxing energies ebbed or surged along the lines, lesser reflective surfaces might become exits and entrances too. Some led nowhere. Others were traps, nasty things lying in wait round blind corners, but some were portals offering glimpses of distant places. People had back doors too, and not just the obvious, also belly button, mouth, nostrils, ear holes, crown of the head, and a point below the point of the big toe of the left foot, worked just as well, though the cranium trapdoor at the back of the skull was harder to prise open.

Of all the people Jake2 tested in the double world, Fatberg's proved the most resistant.

The difficulty he faced was the sheer number of lines passing Fatberg's various backdoors (of which he had no more than any other person) connecting him to people, places, events, and devices. So many indeed radiating Fatberg's backdoors, from the perspective of the double world the lines, a porcupine would have been an apt comparison – only this was one possessed of an infinite number of spines, that extended to the furthest corner of the planet and beyond. Truly, in his physical aspect, the man was a phenomenon. But for Jake2, the biggest puzzle of all was that there didn't seem to be another side to him. Sure he was conniving, duplicitous, and an expert liar – that was evident, in everything he said and did. However, uniquely with Fatberg, what you saw was what you got, and no matter how hard Jake2 had pried, he still hadn't been able to detect so much as a trace of a shadow It lurking in the bristling man.

*

As soon as he stepped down from the Pizza Hut it was obvious to Fatberg that the weird *aumm* sound issued from within the stupa on the summit of the hill. The basso vibration was accompanied by higher frequencies, which set his capped teeth on edge as he walked up the slope towards the whitewashed building, its dome still fluttering with ragged flags, put up without permission, by whoever was making that annoying sound inside.

Perhaps, he speculated, it was a local band, and this was the only place they had to practice their weird *aumm* Nepalese music. Maybe he should pass them onto an A and R producer, on one of his v-record labels? It certainly had something, that deep vibration, impacting his solar plexus, making him feel quite lightheaded as he walked closer. But then, when he was a few feet away from the dark entrance (5 ft., he later estimated) the sound suddenly jumped in volume, and it was like he hit a wall, and he could go no further.

Was it a force-field, he wondered, testing it for breaches with his hands.

Who was responsible? Perhaps it was a secret weapon of the Nepalese Military. If so, he would protest at the highest level to their government. This was his property.

After circling the stupa several times in an anticlockwise direction, and still being kept away by the invisible wall, Fatberg retreated back to his Pizza Hut, to mull the problem over.

Yet he later decided to ignore the stupid stupa, and the dumb Nepalese music, which were only a distraction from his most tricky problem – namely Carrie, and what to do about her …

*

CHAPTER 2

Batbox conversation on <small>small</small> talk: 02.01. hrs, 9/10/43.

'Hey D'lish, what's new?'

'Not much this end, Grimepappa. Reliving the teens I never had in the latest 90's v-peat, is about it. You?'

'The biggest blockbuster ever! The Great Olympus Games, up on Mount Olympus with the gods.'

'Wow!'

'You have to catch it livestream before it goes to v-ries.'

'Who you playin'?'

'A god.'

'That figures. Who?'

'Prometheuz.'

'Sexy?'

'What do you think? (laughs) He's a god!'

'Handsome?'

'You bet. Total hunk. Superpowers, all

that. You'd love him.'

'Sounds like. When can we meet?'

(laughs) 'He's the youngest god. Real cheeky. Loves his mom but don't get on with his daddy, who's real bad, like you can't imagine. Been great playin' in his skin so far, but won't last I can tell.'

'You reckon?'

'Yea, trouble ahead. Expect, big, black clouds, bubbling up, everywhere, to boil a planet in a hot broth of Flashin' lightnin', crashin' thunder, floods. All that. Yea. My big bad daddy god, beatin' up my sweet mommy god, above those weeping, roiling clouds. Up in Mount Olympus, all my sister gods and brother gods giving me grief, like I'm to blame ...'

Her stiletto heels clicking on the treads of a rolling strip mill designed to replicate the sounds and sensations of movement of any number of environments, Rhea, the Mother of the gods, was very annoyed indeed. The strip mill was, in this case, replicating the flagstones of an echoing passageway leading into a labyrinth of tunnels, cored into a 70,00 foot high non-fungible cliff.

The fact that until recently all the gods in her charge had been unemployed actors subsisting on BRED was neither here nor there. Until you stepped off set (passed through that that minor delirium no one ever admitted to), while in character they were gods and should act accordingly, and not go off-script, as one of them just had. Livestream verities were as real as you made them, and belief was the most important constituent in passing on that special shared 'reality' to the audience, who after all became participants in real-time, or whenever they replayed the verity.

She was angry because the actor playing her young son Prometheuz had refused to go against the will of Zeus, the father of the gods. Even as a child, Zeus was a monster, when but a little boy he killed both of his parents, the last of the Titans, so ending their reign in heaven. Then, becoming a father, he devoured the first eight of their children soon as they were born, standing, grinning at her, smacking his ruddy lips behind his bloodied beard, after snacking on their tender flesh like they were suckling piglets, belching and spitting out their chewed bones (which ever after circled Heaven, far out beyond the orbit of Saturn, later known as the Cuiper Belt of asteroids and occasionally raining down judgement on unsuspecting mortals). That was before she made the tunnel labyrinth, where she hid when giving birth. The birth chamber itself was located in his one blind spot, directly below his throne on the lofty summit of Mount Olympus, from where he surveyed the whole of creation.

At a relatively safe distance from Zeus's terrible rages, but conveniently placed in Rhea's view, lay the nursery planet where infant immortals were confined until of an age to fend for themselves in Olympus. There, sibling rivalry was fierce. Being the youngest god by several millennia, Prometheuz, although no longer an infant, had the planet all to himself. As such, none of his older sisters or brothers were around to warn him not to breathe life into the manikins he had shaped from clay-dough in the play pit which, in a far distant future, would be known as Africa. The new creatures were fast breeders, and before long they were spreading across the small world, trailing destruction behind them.

When Zeus heard what Prometheuz had done, he was furious. Breath was life, and by bestowing his on these creatures he had given them consciousness, which up till then had been an attribute of the gods alone.

But Prometheuz, who was the most stubborn of Zeus's children, then enraged his father still further, by pleading to be allowed to give his new playmates fire because it was cold down in the nursery, and the little humans, as he called the creatures he had created, did not have the means to heat themselves.

Zeus had heard enough. Summoning all the gods to his great hall, he then issued one of his famous edicts.

'Fire,' he thundered, 'is the sole property of the gods, for it is one of the four sacred elements from which everything is composed. The knowledge of how to make it must remain ours and ours alone, till the end of eternity. For should these vermin which Prometheuz has willfully created, or any other mortal creature, ever learn the secrets of making the sacred element, then at some time distant in the future Olympus itself might be overthrown.'

He paused, noticing that pillars of the hall had started shaking, threatening to bring the vast roof crashing down on the bowed heads of the assembled gods. Moderating his tone slightly, he continued, 'This I have seen in the tapestry of the heavens, which as every god knows contains all possible pasts and futures, in the weft and woof of the omnipresent-verse.'

But that was precisely the outcome Rhea most fervently desired. And so, when her youngest son, Prometheuz, upon whom her hopes of liberation from the rule of her despotic husband now depended, refused her secret command to steal fire from the sacred flame which perpetually flickered in the hearth of Zeus's Great Hall, she didn't know what to do. The prospect of submitting to her husband's will forever and ever, which meant being regularly raped in their marital bed, or elsewhere for that matter, then bearing an endless succession of children who only grew up to despise her, was one she could not countenance.

And besides, unless Prometheuz did as he was told, there would be no story, no blockbuster verity telling of the twilight of the gods, followed by the rise and fall and rise again of humanity. It was the building of civilizations from Gilgamesh, Nineveh, Babylon, and ziggurats of Mesopotamia, when Sargon ruled the Middle East, the Pyramids in Egypt, the ancient Greeks, the empire of Alexander the Great, Carthage and the Punic wars, with the Roman empire, the Tang dynasty in China, the corresponding civilizations in the Americas, the European renaissance, the Industrial Revolution, before the modern age, and rise of the American Empire, and the great digital age that elevated the super-rich to titan status, at last bringing the epic up-to-date, when one Titannaire would consume all the others and the great cosmic cycle could begin again. Without it, all the actors, herself included, would all too soon be again subsisting on BRED, a prospect she could not abide.

Whereas, for Prometheuz, who, if he agrees, in the next episode will be sentenced by his father to be chained to a rock on Mount Caucusus on planet Earth, where he played as a child. There he would have his liver eaten by an eagle by day, only for it to regrow overnight and endure the same, in the following X number of episodes of the livestream verity. It was a prospect he could not, *would not*, agree to, as he had made abundantly clear to his divine mother.

The new inductee was perfect for the part, the producer and the team all agreed, but only after they got the message without being told – that no more delay will be tolerated…

So it was decided, on a whim and nod at the very top, descending through the vital but nevertheless non-specific order descending the 10 C-title ranks of corporate structure, from the Chief executive officer, to the Chief of Information Officer, then via the Board, to Chief of Staff, the Vice Chairman, Director, Associate Director, Vice Presidents, and down through the 20 subdivisions of Middle Management.

It was passed on, in shrugs and winks, sometimes with words appended to flesh out body language, till it was finally received and understood well enough, though not without a few grumbles from the bottom feeders behind the scenes. But no matter. Despite the new player's obvious total lack of experience, and grumbles aside, the production team were all compliant and got on with preparations for the next episode without protest. For every link in that corporate command chain knew that to do otherwise would have damaged their career prospects across an integrated network of companies, most being prime movers in their respective fields of commerce and industry – whether in construction, housing, property management, insurance, finance and debt recovery, autonomous delivery and transport, satellite launchers, virtual travel, news and entertainment (which of course came under the new heading of V-media), citizen security, remote policing, homeless welfare, and enforcing the provision of the new universal mental health legislation. Such was the connectivity of the giant corporation across the piste, as the saying went in the shut-in world.

*

Jake frowned. As far as he remembered, the schemata of the subs, which he'd worked on for all those months, only had 12 levels, yet the illuminated panel above the shiny steel doors had just signaled 13, indicating that the rapid transit elevator was still descending.

'Not much further now,' George George said, perhaps sensing Jake's confusion.

'How deep does this go?' Jake said, as the elevator slowed and 23 glowed on the screen.

'All the way!' George George said, with a shudder. 'Believe me, you don't want to know. The lower levels,' he added, pointing a finger down at the floor, 'have been reserved for our more hopeless cases.

Fortunately,' he smiled lopsidedly, 'presently, we don't have too many of those, but that will change.'

'I see,' Jake said, becoming more confused as the doors opened onto a vast space.

Dim illumination was provided by emergency lighting panels spaced at hundred or so yard intervals along the intensely black walls. The dim light from below reflected off the undersides of a multitude of shiny rails, which with his architectural knowledge Jake instantly recognized as the latest in malev lighting tracks, which were suspended from a network of gantries high above. The floor below was scattered with equipment, the purpose of most of which he could only guess at. Some four hundred yards distant, as far as he could judge, halfway between the two walls to the side, a raised circular area occupying the center of the space suggested a stage, on which were free-standing L-shapes, curves, and half-circles, that appeared to be constructed with the same light-absorbing material as the walls were.

'Fabulous, isn't it!' George George said into the vastness, which seemed to swallow his voice, like ink spilled on blotting paper, with no reverb whatsoever from the distant walls.

'But what is it?' Jake said, peering into the darkness, which seemed to stretch infinitely ahead.

'What you are looking at, Mr Cousins,' George George beamed, lopsidedly, 'is only the biggest, the best, the most costly and futuristic verity studio in the whole world.'

'But why so large?'

'Aha!' George George raised a long finger, knobbly and bent, 'Very good question, Mr Cousins. That's so it can accommodate a cast of thousands.'

'How is that legal,' Jake interjected, 'when for the past three years under the emergency regulations meetings of more than two people have been forbidden?'

'There are always exemptions, Mr Cousins,' George George assured him, blandly.

'Such as?' Jake insisted.

'Well, the subs, as you call them,' George George said, seemingly surprised by the question.

'That's only because they provide emergency housing,' Jake snapped. 'But this…' He gestured at the surroundings. 'This is to do with the entertainment industry. There's no exemption for that, surely.'

'Aha,' George George wagged that finger, 'but the regulations only extend sixty feet below ground, or three floors, whichever is greater. As the esteemed designer of the, ah, subs, I had assumed you would be aware of that.'

'But what about the dangers of the dust, for instance those manic attacks people can have after inhaling it.' Jake, who up to then had been a sceptic about the potential side-effects, was suddenly wondering if inhaling the toxic dust during his one or other of his excursions on the roof of the Pierspoint, had brought on his recent episode (forgetting of course, he'd only been an onlooker, as his iteration smashed every device in apartment).

'Be reassured, Mr Cousins, at this depth below ground, and breathing charcoal-filtered air as we are, there is, ah, no particulate risk whatsoever posed by the deadly Siberian dust. We are entirely safe here, I promise, which would not be the case obviously if, ha hah, the studio were, um, above ground.'

'I have understood that,' Jake said, becoming impatient with George George's long winded explanations. 'Please, could you expand about this cast of thousands.'

'Ah yes, the cast. Well, ah, first there is the actual cast, the ah, real-live actors, so to speak, and then there is the, um crowd of, um, avatars, I believe that is the correct name?'

'The perps,' Jake said, more to himself.

'The what?' George George peered intently at Jake.

'Sorry, of course I mean the avatars.'

'Indeed,' George George nodded gravely.

'Where do they go?' Jake insisted.

'Is it not obvious?' George George expostulated, 'in the stands, of course.'

'What stands? I don't see any,' Jake said, making a show of peering around.

'Oh they are projected.' George George waved a hand, airily. 'Nothing to write home about. Like any amphitheater, but on a scale to accommodate billions only the ascending tiers are each divided into enclosures, which are opened at the end of the show. The stage is in the middle, over there.' He pointed. 'But there is no proper set, as you might expect in a play or a movie, just crosses and grids marked on the floor, and the ah higgledy piggledy structures that the technicians tell me will be granite furniture, temple walls, and altars, and so forth.' He paused, and turned towards Jake. 'Am I going on too long?' He swept back a lank lock of hair that had fallen over his eyes. 'It's a bad habit of mine, I'm told.' He looked down.

'I guess V-tech production is *confusing*,' Jake said, glad he had stopped himself before saying 'alarming', and suppressing a desire to laugh.

George George sighed. 'Things were much more straightforward in my time, and of course done very differently. However I do understand that these days the participating avatars prime the pump, so to speak, and are considered essential to the financing of big production serials.' He raised a finger. 'But that is when the, ah, subs, enter the picture.'

'I was wondering when you'd get round to that.' Jake smiled.

'Yes, we provide real-life extras, when needs be,' George George said, with evident pride. 'Also, when needed, a back-up crew, as it were, who assist all the support staff that livestream big budget verities require nowadays.'

'But there's no one here,' Jake said, looking around to make a point.

'That's because they are, ah, preparing for the next episode, Mr Cousins.'

'So where is this emergency you need my help with?' Jake said, with the odd thought that the studio was the same number of floors below ground as the roof of the Pierspoint was above it.

'That, I have to admit, Mr Cousins,' George George said, squinting down his nose sheepishly at him, 'was just a ploy to get you down here.' He smiled lopsidedly. 'So what do you think?'

'Great.' Jake shrugged, realizing that he was only 23 floors underground because of all his code 307 violations up on the roof, where he'd inhaled the toxic dust, in another life which was now fading like a dream. 'Very impressive, yea. But I don't know what it has to do with me.'

'Ah ha.' George George raised a finger. 'But that's where you are wrong,' he said, emphatically. 'This has *everything* to do with you.' He shook his head, sadly. 'If only I was younger, I might have had stood an outside chance.' He sighed, deeply. 'But instead, they have chosen you.' He extended a hand. 'Truly, it is, ah, the greatest honor of my life to be the first to congratulate you on your, ah, marvelous good fortune.' Overdoing the dramatics, George George placed his other hand over his heart. 'Believe me when I say that I shall always remember this moment.'

Observing the exchange from a distant location, Jake2 smiled darkly to himself, knowing full well what came next for his unfortunate body double.

*

CHAPTER 3

Conversation on the FauxReel Culture Vultures Channel: 15:hrs. 11/10/43.

'Elliot, is that really you under that basket of writhing snakes?'

'Yes Petronella, it truly is. I have finally changed my allegiances from avian to monster. This is my new avatar. Humungous doesn't begin to address the new Me, don't you think?'

'Ghastly! I hardly dare look.'

'Afraid of being turned to stone?'

'Hardly! That would make me a Roc.'

'Very funny. I'm in character, for the next episode. Two hours to go. I can't wait.'

'Me too, though I can't see what connection Medusa of the Perseus legend has with Prometheuz.'

'Oh come on, the Ancient Greeks were always mixing their myths. You know that.'

'That's like conflating Adam and Eve

with Samson and Delilah, which I think you'll find I am correct in saying comes three hundred and twenty-two chapters on in the Bible.'

'You always were so picky, Petronella.'

'Just making a point, Elliot. Prometheuz and his conflict with his almighty father, Zeus, was the Ancient Greeks' creation myth, just as for us the legend of the Fall is, in the Old Testament.'

'Testament, now that's an interesting word, don't you think?'

'So like you to try changing the subject when you know I'm right, Elliot.'

'Not at all, Petronella. Testament is derived from testicle, because no one believed those Biblical Patriarchs unless they cupped theirs when swearing oaths. The word's absolutely fundamental to Western Civilization.'

'Maybe for you, Elliot, but certainly not for me!

'You are so right, Petronella. Vultures like you don't have 'em!'

*

Concealed by thick smog, the Pizza Hut's containment field's stabilizers, embedded in its seven sides, ensured the craft remained more or less stationary at 15.3 feet above the building, with a deviation either side of just 0.012 inches, as measured by the on-board optical instrumentation as it hovered over the roof of the Pierspoint.

However, unusually, Fatberg wasn't thinking of any of that, nor did he pause to consider as he descended the steps – or even to count them as otherwise habitually he would have done – that in a FauxReel studio, 23 levels under the Firebrick site, the much-heralded livestream episode, coincidentally also numbered 23, of the biggest blockbuster was about to begin. Instead, he was anxiously wondering what sort of reception awaited him in the apartment directly below.

When Carrie heard the ceiling hatch in the hall outside her workroom sliding back, then saw the roof ladder extending towards the floor, she thought she was dreaming. Jake was locked away in the subs, so how come he was clambering down the ladder, into the apartment? But then, with a flash of anger, she recognized who it was.

'Julius, how the hell …?' 'Please.' He held up his hands. 'I only had one chance to come here without being observed and that is today, when everyone's attention is elsewhere.'

'And what's so special about today?' she demanded, hands on hips, glowering.

'Only the biggest grossing verity of all time.' He glanced at his watch, paused, then looked up. 'In precisely nine minutes and twenty seconds, the two singing comperes will start the countdown to episode twenty-three of the Great Olympus Games show, or the GO Games as it has become known.'

'Oh that.' Carrie shrugged. 'I never participate.'

'Billion already are, just everyone in the city will be streaming – apart from you.' He laughed, covering up his nervousness, before adding, in a pleading tone, 'And me.'

'Hmm.' Carrie, who was not long out of the shower and still in her dressing gown, uncrossed her arms and relaxed her stance. 'Well, it's good to have you here at last, Julius.' She half smiled. 'But I still don't understand why you couldn't give me some warning.'

'It was a last minute snap decision I could only make when I could be sure that the smog had thickened enough to conceal the hut from being seen from below.'

'Ok, I finally understand.' Smiling, she spread her arms and motioned with her hands. 'Come on, give me a hug. I think I need it as much as you do, Julius.'

*

'Please try not to move, you need to let these gorgeous rectus abdominis muscles settle-in or they won't bond properly, Prometheuz, sir.'

'How many times do I have to tell you, my name is Cousins, not Prometheuz,' Jake protested, weakly.

'Of course, Mr, ah, Cousins,' the body therapist hastily corrected herself, as she leaned over him. 'It's just with these muscles, I can't help thinking of you as Prometheuz, who I have followed from the beginning. I admit I was totally devastated when I heard the last actor had walked out on the set. But quite honestly I find you so much more impressive, and I know that you'll soon win the audience over.' She sighed happily as she applied creams to his tender new flesh, of what he had previously thought of as his abs, as he lay, a mask on his face, under the bright lights of the make-up suite, into which he had been wheeled, strapped to the cantilevered bed, some minutes before.

'May I say they've done a tremendous job in the Lab. This maximus glutinous is absolutely outstanding,' she went on, carefully avoiding the prominent bump of his gauze-wrapped genitals, which were particularly tender, moving her hands down to his thighs. 'Since I began here, Mr Prom –sorry, Mr Cousins – seven months ago, though it seems an age, just before the first sensational episode of The First Family when Zeus ate the triplet godlings his poor wife had just given birth to and the whole world got hooked, I've made-up all the Olympians, who all went through the same procedure, and let me tell you, none of them looked half so god-like after their ordeal ...'

As she chattered on, this time about the distortion lenses they projected on the set, Jake was desperately trying to recall one of the bedtime stories his grandfather had read to him from the Book of Greek Legends when he was a small child. But it was no use. Despite his best efforts, the details of what happened to the hero escaped him. He needed to remember in order to work out what came next. But his lines the silly voice coach (who confusingly kept calling him Prometheuz) had recited to him earlier, all the time looping round the wheelchair in her rollerblades while an orderly, who he never saw pushed him up the ramp, told him very little. Besides, the words she had made him endlessly repeat were all jumbled up in his head by the time they reached the top, where a lizard lawyer in a sharp suit, with creases that could have cut paper, stood waiting before rubber double doors under a sign that said 'GENOPLAST' in ominous black letters.

From the moment the lawyer took over from the voice coach, who skated away back down the spiral ramp way to the Induction Suite from whence they had just come, lizard legalese never stopped coming out of the near side of the lawyer's motor mouth. He went on about minutiae of a contract which Jake was now required to understand, though he only made out about one word in three, and understood even less, they came so fast. Without a let-up of the monologue, the lawyer wheeled Jake through the door and into a blue-lit room, where he was told to strip off by a white-coated technician and made to stand against a wall marked with a grid, while different-coloured lights from a hidden source in the ceiling played over his naked body, as another technician traced dotted lines projected onto his skin, outlining different areas of his anatomy, back and front, which most worryingly included his groin, with a big felt-tipped pen.

The only details of the contract that he could now remember, after the 7-hour procedure he had just undergone, were the seven zeros of the 9-figure number, which had made him quite dizzy, when he'd read them. The money to be transferred into an off-shore bank account which had already been opened in his name immediately upon his completing his part in the last episode of the First Family series.

But then, after he signed on the 40th page of the densely worded contract and it had been witnessed by one of the technicians, the lawyer's tone had changed from silk to sandpaper, as he spoke of the dire consequences of being found to be intoxicated while on the set, or, worst of all, if he walked out on and broke his contract, as his predecessor in the role had. In that case, the most egregious penalties of the 192 sanctions as set out in the many sub-clauses of the contract would be applied with the utmost rigor, by the battery of L.A. lawyers which FauxReel kept on hand for just such an eventuality.

With the lawyer's final warning ringing in his ears, and escorted by a honor guard of white-coated technicians, he was propelled upon a trolley through the next set of double doors under a sign that said 'THEATRE' in bold black letters, and into a vast white space which was ablaze with lights, where the purpose of all those mysterious red-dotted lines marked on his anatomy finally became clear.

*

Standing with her back to him, Carrie studied his reflection in the kitchen mirror. Sitting with his hands clenched on the tabletop before him, he was pretending to look around the room, while covertly casting her side glances.

'Black or white?' she cast back over her shoulder.

'Black, please,' he said, their eyes meeting in the mirror, 'I never take it any other way.'

'Sugar?' she asked, smiling.

'No, never.' He laughed nervously. 'Too many calories. I stopped taking it twenty-three months and ...'

Leaning around him, she laid a coaster on the table before him and placed the steaming mug of coffee on top. Standing behind him, her dressing gown brushing his back as she kneaded his shoulders, she said, 'Julius, you're *so* tense.'

'It's been a hard week,' he sighed. 'I've left the team to carry on the negotiation in that dumb cat capital. Sorry, I forget its name. The whole time that spooky monk aumm music playing somewhere. Take it from me, all Neps are nuts. You cannot imagine how stupid ...'

'Julius, forget all that,' she said, settling in her chair. 'You're here.' Reaching over the table and grasping his hands, she unclenched his fingers. 'Safe. With me.'

She settled back in her chair, and regarded him coolly. 'Julius,' she continued, 'you never do anything without a reason, I know, so please tell me what's on your mind.' She arched an elegant eyebrow. 'Unless of course you've lost it, and you really did come all this way for my coffee? I know it's good but not that good, surely.'

'Carrie, I ...' Caught in the spell of her glittering peacock blue eyes, he was unable to look away.

'Go on,' she urged.

'I've been so lonely I ...' His downcast eyes welled, self-piteously.

'Listen, Julius, I won't be able to respect you as a man if you can't tell me. You need to know that. I'm just that sort of woman.'

'Carrie I ...' Suddenly, Fatberg knelt before her. 'Carrie, please, will you consent to be my wife. I promise ...' He gulped, perspiration peppering his forehead. 'I swear, I will always care for you.'

Intent, she studied his upturned face, secretly glad that at least he hadn't mentioned love because, as she had lately learned, that only got in the way of survival in a cruel world. Knowing she was losing Jake in that moment, she took a deep breath, and smiled.

'Yes.' She clasped the hand which Julius extended. 'But on one condition.'

'Condition?' – *was that a petulant frown, Jake2, who was remote viewing the scene, wondered.*

'Our marriage must be kept secret.'

'But I imagined ...'

'No, Julius, the ceremony has to be totally private. There must be no press intrusion whatsoever or you can forget it.'

'I agree! Yes, totally, absolutely!' he exclaimed, jumping to his feet.

'In that case, Julius, you may now kiss me.'

Watching from afar and near, Jake2 was pleased.

Now that their lifelines, on which he had been focused, were twined and soon to be knotted, at last he could advance his plans in other directions. Since he had come into actualized existence he had learned that any form of stasis, such as he had just endured to bring together the two people in the apartment below where he was bi-located, sitting cross-legged on the old rooftop watertank, posed innumerable risks for him, just as they would any of the other elementals who flitted between the double world and its earthly counterpart. They were half-life beings, which like him were composed of more energy than substance and were never one thing nor another, but so much more free than the shut-in denizens of either world.

CHAPTER 4

The PERP-VOX PEEP Show-*Scoops all the poop between the scenes.*

'Oh there you are, Petronella, dearest. With so many of your kind here today, it was hard to make you out in that flock.'

'I would have spotted you anywhere in that ghastly hissing headdress. And anyway, Elliot, or should I say, *my dear* Medusa, the correct term for a gathering of more than three vultures is "kettle".'

'I never knew that, would you credit it?'

'Yes, I would. Before you turned feather, you were always a most laggardly raptor.'

'Really?'

'Yes, and besides, I was in a minority of one over there.'

'So my new snake eyes were deceiving me, were they?'

'Aside from the fact I was chatting to one of the three bald eagles in the carrion stand, I believe I am correct in saying I am the only representative of my ancient genus of vulture here today.'

'And what is that, pray?'

'The nephhron percnioptrous genus, more commonly known as the Egyptian Vulture.'

'Thank you for enlightening me at last, dearest.'

'These days, we are quite rare, you know.'

'Yes, I can see that.'

'We were worshipped as divine in Ancient Egypt.'

'I am sure you were, Petronella. And got to eat pharaohs' entrails too, I imagine.'

'Only after their other body parts had been properly mummified.'

'Of course. And today?'

'We live in hope, my dear Medusa, but with so many pay-2-perp avatars present, I am afraid I don't rate my chances highly, if at all.'

'Tsk, tsk, Petronella. Such gloom is not at all like you. I am sure the other vultures will save you a juicy morsel or two.'

'I wouldn't for them, so why should they?'

'Not even for a divine nephhron percnioptrous?'

'Absolutely not. That would be to forego half the pleasure.'

'More than the ravening and tearing?' *(sighs)* 'I used to love that.'

'Perhaps not, but even so, flying away with the last gibbet in one's beak is always particularly satisfying.'

'Quite so.' *(looks up)* 'Ah, but do I detect the lights are finally dimming?'

'I do believe you are correct, yes. And look at those screens. No, not over there, Elliot, that direction.' *(points a wingtip)* 'At last the colonnades of Olympus are pixelating into view. About time. And the stars of Heaven twinkling beyond. Do you see, on the screens there?'

'Ah, so they are. Marvellous. As always, dearest, your eyesight is spot on.'

'None better. Certainly I wouldn't trust any of yours.' *(laughs)*

'But only my looks can turn to stone, dearest.'

'Not my prey, please, dear Medusa.'

'I wouldn't dare.' *(laughs)* 'Well, to our separate places then, Petronella dearest.'

'Please give my regards to your new kin in the monster stand.'

'Will do, oh divine one, and most assuredly my fellow gorgons will be delighted to receive them. See you after the show, offal permitting.' *(laughs, walks away)*

*

In the Observation Deck, leaning on the rail, Carrie peered down at the roof of the Pierspoint, as it was swallowed by smog.

Would she ever see Jake again, she wondered? Given recent events, she doubted it. Fate, in her experience, was cruel far more often than it was kind. The great wheel of fortune she remembered so vividly from her Granmama's worn deck of cards had turned, and what they'd had would never return – not in this life, anyway, she reflected, not now she was on her way to her secret wedding in Kathmandu.

The past three years with Jake had been the most stable period in her whole life, and the apartment the first real home she'd ever known. Amazingly, despite the long shut-in and her terror whenever the building swayed in the wind, and the fear that never left her because of the height of the tower block, she'd actually been happy most of the time, even though Jake was the most annoying person she'd ever known. But of all his behaviours his foolish arrogance in believing that he could forever get away with flouting the emergency regulations had finally brought disaster down on both of them, and now he was suffering the consequences for his escapes onto the roof.

In a way she blamed herself for not coming down harder on him when she first discovered what he was up to and nipping his behaviors in the bud. But then, reconsidering, she realized he had been hell-bent all along and she could have done nothing to stop him. Poor Jake, how he hated to be confined.

Sobbing silently, she tried to conjure his face out of the fog, knowing then that, despite her anger, she still loved him. What was he thinking of, locked in his cell at that moment? Was he regretting what he had done? Or was he relieved to be free of her nagging, which he was always complaining of, and glad to be finally shot of her? Wiping away the great fat tear that suddenly coursed down her cheek, she wondered if she would ever know happiness again.

Don't look back, never look back, she told herself, steeling herself against the almost overwhelming compulsion to break down and sob her eyes out lest Julius, up in the cockpit, overhear her. She stared into the smog which had swallowed up her past with Jake so completely. Don't look back, never look back. Yea, John's mantra during her childhood years, when to keep ahead of the bad guys they had to move every couple of months, and move countries every two or three years, till they reached New Zealand, after which there was nowhere else to go.

But despite all his care and the precautions he took, they still got him in the end. Then, twelve years later, when she thought they had lost the trail, and she was safe at last, they would have killed her too if Julius hadn't been watching over her. If only he could have warned her about the danger earlier – but even so, he deserved her loyalty, for without his presence of mind at the time and placing those two guard bots in the corridor outside the apartment, she'd be well dead by now. Jake too, since he was standing before her and would have opened the door to the assassin. Too bad he went mad after and wrecked the apartment. But at least by so doing, he decisively ended their relationship, leaving her no other alternative than to go forwards without him.

Though Julius was a cold fish, he clearly cared. But even more importantly considering her perilous present situation, he was rich and powerful enough to protect her from the malevolent force that had been behind the murder of three generations of her family, which she had no doubt still had her in its sights. That the assassins were only instruments of a dark design had long been obvious to her, but now she wasn't even convinced there was a human face in the center of its web, which she sensed was alien in what she could only think of as its essential *wrongness.* Not just her entire family had been wiped out to advance its plans of world domination and total subjection of the planet's entire population. In its name (if indeed it had a name), empires had been toppled, terrible wars had been waged on land and sea and in every corner of the world (and soon above it, if the stand-off in space between the great powers broke down, as looked increasingly likely, and the recent militarization of the lunar surface was anything to go by), while in Russia tens of millions had been murdered, whether by starvation, in forced marches, frozen in Siberian gulags, injected by doctors with weird serums, in medical experiments, or tortured to death by brutal militia, state thugs or soft-spoken KGB killers.

In China too, the story had been much the same under Mao's reforming zeal, except there, if anything, the death toll had been even greater, during the 'great leap forwards' of the 1970's. It was a game, Granmama had explained, which was played by both ends against the middle, where the people always lost no matter which side won. Just as in World War II, at the conclusion of which allegiances and the uniforms changed but the rules stayed the same, and the principal victors remained hidden behind the scenes. Blood-sucking Capitalism and Communism, she said, were bedfellows as hard to tell apart as any two fleas under a blanket.

Considering any of the previous, self-pity wasn't even an option. She was who she was, and if she wanted to retain any self-respect, ultimately she had no choice but to accept the role that history had placed on her shoulders. Like it or not she was the Tsarina, and now that, by proposing, Julius had pledged his implicit support in her cause, who was she to argue against him or indeed the prayers of her long-suffering subjects, whom Granmama had often spoke of. Ever since she remembered, their wrinkled faces had intruded in her dreams, the mad mystics with burning eyes and great flowing white beards, always with crosses on the long black robes they wore over hair shirts, and their mortified flesh they regularly scourged with flails – if Granmama was to be believed. The ragged bent old women in headscarves, shawls slung across bony shoulders, down on their knees on slabs of cold stone, bowing before icons of saints, and heretics in the dimness of onion-domed churches in old Mother Russia, where she had never been, but which was always at the back of her mind. Yea, all those poor oppressed people she had too long turned her back on, their pleading voices following her down the years as, seeking anonymity, she hid, tried to blend into the background wherever she was.

But now, with the clarion call of destiny resounding more urgently than ever in the depths of her being, perhaps she should actually be grateful to Jake for pushing her towards it. Instead of nursing resentments, she should let him go. People weren't possessions, and love that didn't turn into contentment never lasted, always turned to poison. Didn't Granmama tell her that? Or maybe it was something she read somewhere. Whatever, the words rang true. She needed to release the caged bird of their love tangled in her heart-strings and set Jake free, for if she did not the black seeds already lodged there would bear bitter fruit in the years to come. Besides, though not in name, she was the Tsarina in her mind already, if she was honest with herself, so what choice did she have?

Ping went the heart-string, as her connection with Jake finally snapped. She never saw that, but her iteration – the yet-to-be Tsarina of her secret dreams – did.

Jake2, who had dropped in on Carrie and her secret self from where he was bi-located in the Great Hall of Zeus, watched the poor heartstring's fraying end whiplashing away as it spiraled into the infinite depths of a shimmering vortex and vanished into null-time. He would have liked to have shared how it looked from his perspective, but there was no point, neither Carrie nor her iteration would have registered anything, trapped as they were in the world of blinding reflections where, no matter where you are, nothing is as it seems except, sometimes, what is glimpsed in fleeting impressions, or gleaned in dreams.

*

THE GREAT OLYMPUS GAMES – SCENE # 2 EPISODE 23

Waiting at the foot of the stairs, listening to the yells and catcalls of the restive crowd above, muscle-weary after his genoplast transformation from man into god, Prometheuz, as Jake was now starting to think of himself, had an attack of the shakes. Despite the repeated assurances from his body therapist, and his rollerblading voice coach, he doubted he would ever get used to the added mass of his sore new muscles. Even the short walk from the cosmetic suite to below the stage had exhausted him.

'Fuck this shit,' he cursed as the insistent clamor climaxed in a rabid roar followed by tidal waves of chanting, peaking, crashing from all sides, on the stage of fake dreams.

'PROM! PROM! PROM! PROM! PROM! PROM! PROM!'

The raucous chanting climaxed in a colossal wall of sound. His head bowed, Prometheuz stepped up onto the stage. Then, registering that the new chants of "GO-PROM GO! GO-PROM-GO! GO-PROM-GO" were directed at him, he flung up his hands, receiving the adulation of the pay-2-perps he could just make out beyond the great pillars of Zeus's great hall, which marked the division of light into darkness. Four times he wheeled about, muscles rippling; the roars only got louder, and as he moved his head to face in a new direction, the non-fungible pillars in his line of sight flickered.

He also registered the same effect in his peripheral vision, where the flicker revealed the giant furniture to be non-fungibles positioned on props.

Not so the pay-2-perp avatars packed into the steep stands, none of whom noticed a single flicker in the beamed blacklight-distorting fields, in between the pillars, which were distorting lenses, basically, which in deft perspective shifts ensured no pillar was ever in the way. The zoom function of the distortion field brought the action closer to the perps live-streaming in their v-consoles who were afforded a 360-view of any god or thing anywhere on the vast stage brought right up to their eyes, simply by willing the command to a sender in their headsets, a trick which was soon acquired after a few ejaculations, when masturbating during gory scenes.

Within the ring of towering pillars, the benches of the defense and prosecution were arranged in a half-circle facing the dock isolated in the middle, in turn dwarfed by the high chair of the judge, the fleece of a golden ram, draped over the back. There was a granite gravel resting on the broad right arm of the empty high chair, which, like the rest of the monumental furniture, was cut from massive blocks of polished stone of an inky blackness that seemed to possess infinite depths. The only exceptions to this stone rule: a great bronze sword and a pair of golden shackles attached to the chunky links of a coil of a solid gold chain on the table next to a massive mace, which was big as a plank, only it was round and had a great crystal boss at one end, of a green that seemed supernatural, its glittering depths drew the eye so.

'Great great entrance, Bro,' someone said, from behind. Turning his head in the direction, Prometheuz spotted a big satyr, who seemed familiar somehow and was stuffed into a lurid green body suit two sizes too small for his gangly frame, striding up to him, wearing the red cloak of a public defender slung over his cuirass and armored shoulder.

Most of the gods Prometheuz had seen so far, wore togas, and none exposed hairy knees and gold hooves. From what he knew of the script he guessed this was supposed to be his older brother in Olympus, and the god of inebriation, fertility, and secret pleasures.

'Bro, I'm DPD that's Dionysus P Dionysus, your ah court appointed defence attorney. Never mind the P.' Dionysus shrugged, 'our mother and her fancies,' he grinned lopsidedly.

'It would help if I knew what I'm charged with,' Prometheuz, managed, helpless with the god's spade hand gripping his bicep, as he was propelled down an aisle between the rows of benches.

'Oh, Zeus's usual trumped-up nonsense,' Dionysus said with difficulty, stooping slightly as he reached two grimy fingernails into his mouth, and pried out a quid of black shag of which he had a regular supply from a dwarf. 'Believe me Bro,' he said, 'there's no fucking case to answer.' Still firmly gripping Prometheuz by the arm, he palmed the gunk into his other hand and slapped it to the back of a bench, as they passed. Straightening up with a wince, he turned his head, and grinned at a statuesque God standing with a trident among a group of demi-gods, settling in further along the bench.

The giant with the trident had little wriggling electric fish tangled in his flowing purple hair, which might have been seaweed, Jake thought, but at that distance it was hard to tell. He had a great beard, with green streaks, down to his knees, boots so deep they could have been pacific lagoons, tropical fish about his knees, as Jake would have expected, since this was obviously the god Poseidon before him, with a seaweed cape slung stylishly across a great shoulder. He was giving Jake the once over.

The eyes of a god can shoot daggers.

'The charge is totally trumped up, and beyond ridiculous!' Dionysus said, his back armored against just such a look, steering Prometheuz in a new course towards the dock directly under Zeus's high chair.

'But what am I charged with?'

Ignoring the question, Dionysus went on, 'And now, with that great entrance, and winning over the crowd which is always half of the battle, Bro, it's positively guaranteed I'll get you off. I fucking swear, believe me, no matter what that stone-eyed fucker up there has planned for you.' Shielding the gesture with his body, Dionysus thumbed towards the high chair, which Prometheuz noticed was now occupied by the massive bulk of a shadowy robed figure with a great head of curly hair, a long beard, and penetrating gleaming eyes that projected ruby-red rays, which he felt as burning heat on his chest as the Father of the Gods glowered down at him.

*

'Change of plan,' Fatberg announced, looking round as Carrie stepped up into the cabin from her suite of rooms on the second deck. 'You'll never guess where now,' he said, with a sly grin, dismissing his scaled-down Appointments Manager with a flick of his fingers.

'I thought you had arranged everything in Kathmandu,' she said, her eyes drawn to the penitent pinstriped avatar, on his little pedestal, which was a cheap non-fungible of St. Theodore's Column outside St. Mark's in Venice, shrinking to nothingness along with his pedestal in a disappearing cone of blacklight, which blipped off in a dot, making her blink. 'I've always wanted to see the Himalayas,' she said, closing her eyes, still seeing the after-image of the dot burning a hole in her retinas.

'We can go there after.' He patted the one other seat next to his in the timber-lined cabin, which was surprisingly small, given the generous space elsewhere in the craft. 'You'd best strap in,' he said, leaning over the lighted instrument panel, 'the forecast is thick smog below, with atmospheric pressure dropping to 12 millibars, and visibility at ground level between 3.5 and 4.2 feet, so we may hit turbulence as we descend.'

Irritated by the sudden change of direction, and still more by his habit of slipping numbers into the conversation that meant nothing to her, *and* wondering where the hell he was taking her now, she stared out of the view screen, where the dot had reappeared on her retinas, this time burning a hole in the clear blue of a cloudless sky. An illusion, which lasted all of a second, when zip – dirty, fraying curtains were slung on a line strung across it. Ditto: smog. This one had a sepia stink, which with the fishscale gloom, invaded the cabin with a briny tang. 'Goddam filters!' Julius snarled, 'Nano's supposed to keep that nasty shit out. You never know what's breeding down here.'

She turned to look at Fatberg, and the burning hole was back, framing his face, but when the cabin lights brightened, the edetic after-image, was gone, though never quite forgotten, for it was a strange moment, and one she would return to, when she first wondered what had possessed her to twine her life with his.

Was she crazy or what? Her impulsive 'yes' to the proposal – which she had wrung out of him (imagine!), sealed with a kiss before she ran into the bedroom and grabbed her ready to go bag from the wardrobe. On the roof, worrying if she'd locked the front door, which was ridiculous because no one but assassins ever called. Then, responding to Julius' urgent summons from above, scrambling up a yellow ladder towards a joke Pizza Hut, which was a seven-sided faux wood cylinder parked in the smog above her, like a fucking party hat. Yes, she'd actually sworn out loud, unforgivable, of course, but she'd been clutching her bag, hanging in the air below the open hatch, where Julius was standing, reaching down a hand, the red and green hazard flashing-lights around him lighting up the smog, like she was back in her teens, in a retro-disco in Rotorooa, New Zealand, when she'd first kissed a boy.

A minute later, the Pierspoint and her life in the apartment was gone, along with the spikes and spires of other tall buildings, and the spider lines of freeways intersecting the city as the Pizza Hut lifted above the smog and Julius set the cruising speed and directions. They had cocktails in the salon, where Julius chatted to the barbot, as the enormity of the change dawned on her.

Sometime later, in her new dressing room, she laid out four outfits on the bed from the rail of designer clothes in the wardrobe.

'Eeney Meeny Miney Mo,' she said, pointing in turn to the Persian Harlot, Tearaway Teen, Serious Secretary …

Perhaps she really would be the Tsarina one day, she reconsidered. She imagined herself in the role as she stood looking at herself in the mirror of her suite of rooms in the most exclusive Pizza Hut in the world, adjusting the mohair brim of her stylish white hat she had picked out from an outfit in the ethnic rail in the wardrobe. Though the tiny print on the label, which had a little picture of a volcano on it, said it was made by the Warranka tribe in Peru, and the round brim wasn't strictly cowgirl, as soon as she saw it, she knew the hat was perfect.

But perfect to whom exactly? she thought. With the hat tipped at a racy angle, the eyes in the face studying her so intently from the mirror seemed to belong to a surreal self who might as well have been a character in a book for all she knew of her, because she was only halfway through reading chapter one of the story. Suddenly, she wanted to be that Carrie, that mysterious other self, which she suspected was as full of surprises as her Granmama's chest of fancy dressing-up clothes from before the Russian Revolution.

'Yes!' she murmured, sealing a secret compact with herself, 'out of the smog, make me the most perfectly surreal Tsarina ever!'

Wondering at her odd mood, half-regretting the wish, and feeling that the universe was shifting to accommodate the pent up feelings she had released with the impulse, she recalled Julius' caution as he'd ushered her from the ladder and into the hatch. He'd said that the containment field of the craft's propulsion drive affected people differently, but not to worry because any effect would soon settle down, though she might feel strange for a while.

A thoughtful expression on her face, she switched off the light in the closet and left the room, the silver heels of her dainty cowgirl boots, which complimented her mix-and-match outfit, clicking on the marble floor tiles as she turned left, towards the crew stairs (a misnomer – there was no crew, none being needed because everything was at the touch of a button, a voice or hand command) rather than the chrome doors of the elevator on the right, which ran up the outside and was basically a glass tube.

What Carrie didn't realize was that the odd interlude when she'd made her fateful wish had not, as she suspected, been brought on by the containment field of the craft's Imp-drive, but rather was the result of a thought string projected into her mind by another Jake, who was standing unseen right beside her at the time.

When Carrie slid open the crew hatch, and stepped down into the cabin, Fatberg was leaning over the retro instrument console, counting under his breath, as he often did when he thought no one was looking.

'Five hundred and twenty, four hundred and ten, three hundred and ninety-two point seven, one hundred and fifteen point two, seventy-five exactly, and ...' He looked up. 'Love the hat, very much, very too much, very, very, very you, moua moua miaow!' For good measure he blew her a kiss. 'Wait for it, wait for it, once again, Tsarina baby,' he chortled, chancing using the pet name he had picked for her – 'Once again, the captain of your heart makes a perfect landing,' he trumpeted.

The Pizza Hut settled down on its airbags, as hundreds, possibly thousands of pigeons disturbed by the sudden landing of the giant craft in the vast, empty square, flew up past the viewscreen.

'Where are we?' she said, disdaining to comment on his latest, stupidest, endearment yet. A cowgirl in a chair sat with one leg extended, and a cowgirl boot heel propped on the console before her, gazing out from under the brim of her new mohair hat at the ghostly outline of a great dome looming out of smog that seemed familiar somehow.

'Don't you recognize it?'

'For your sake I hope you've not brought us back in a circle?' she said, sitting up. But then her ready scowl was replaced by an expression of astonishment. As the swirling smog thinned a little, her jaw dropped, and she saw that the soaring dome did not, as she had first assumed, belong to a large, very controversial shopping mall a few miles from the apartment she had recently vacated, but instead was the dome and the two wings of the original edifice which the mall's profile exactly replicated – an ancient place of worship that was of supreme importance to a significant proportion of the population of the planet.

But rather less so for their iterations who, whether lucid or otherwise, rarely attach the same significance to objects as do their corporeal counterparts in the world of material existence, who whether believers or not, by dint of their physicality are inevitably so much more bound to place than are their other selves.

Iterations such as Jake2, who watched with amusement from his perch on a pink granite obelisk in the middle of the square, which at 25.12 m stood a mere .12 m higher than the Pizza Hut parked beside it. A metal ramp extended from the craft's lower deck and a little white bubble car, designed like a toy spaceship with wheels, just the passengers' heads showing under the perspex dome, one sitting straight-backed with the brim of her hat downturned. The other's head was bobbing, a hand gesticulating, as he drove down into the square around the obelisk, till he got a bearing, when he turned and proceeded in the direction of the great basilica.

A word here about the Pizza Hut's Imppulse drive.

He had already forgotten its dumb name, but the big number got Fatberg's attention after the hopeful had stood up and started his 5-minute pitch at the penultimate Invent-slam, events FakeReal had held in cities across the country back in the day, when the company was just a glorified start-up. Now, if he had understood right from the big guy in the spot, each second, the Universe manifested a total of 229,879,856,798,722,765.32 times.

Recognizing in the inventor a fellow counter, Fatberg then asked him,

'What do you do with all the numbers?'

'Null time,' the man, whose name Fatberg could never remember, (even though his squashed face with his car mats for eyebrows, and snarled black eyes that sometimes haunted him on the edge of sleep), had said, 'that's where I put 'em. In the Drawer of Infinite Depth, hidden in Null-space between each one of them pulses. Skip a drawer, flip a pulse, in the big M number, rich man,' (as, from the start he had called Fatberg) 'and there you have the impulse.'

Pointing to a dial on the portable Imp-drive he had brought with him, he continued,

'Adjust the pulse with this, and the seven phase containment field jumps any which way. No energy required. Simple! It's all done by dampening the oscillation of these finely tuned titanium plates here, and upping the oscillations on the other six plates to catch the Null-energy surge, at the next non-manifestation, when the pulse skips a beat between Fibonacci sequences of the big M number. Neat, huh? Up pulsing I call it, though it really should be described as up-down-side-pulsing, and compensating interface energy displacement. The principal being, rich man, move the field, and anything you put in the field moves too.

Some small objects from the pockets of the panel were then moved in the air, in their respective confinement fields.

Questions followed.

Asked to expand on the operating principal, the inventor, said, 'Nothin' to it, rich man.' He shrugged. 'S'all 'bout switching push and resistance, between these here seven plates, which when scaled up can be embedded in any size of structure. While over here,' he said, reaching out a finger to sketch an invisible border about a foot from the small generator, which he said was approximated to the relative distance to size ratio of three over five, between the seven plates. 'Where the smaller containment field interfaces with the great universal one, which naturally is a whole lot bigger.'

It was at this point that the moderator intervened as, laughing at a joke no one else got, the inventor took out a chewed cheroot, which was later found to contain illegal substances, lit up, and released a great gust of smoke in which he was quickly removed by security, who were already in attendance (having been alerted by concerned members of the audience).

But he had said enough for Fatberg to be convinced. There was enough method in the madness, that when Fatberg caught up with the beat-up schmuck on the sidewalk outside, where security had tossed him a minute before, he offered his hand, before shaking on another fabulous FakeReal Associate deal.

This was despite the sucker's pitch being quite the worst in the invent-slam nationwide tour, which took in 17 identical conference centers in as many cities. It all soon blended into one dreary city, wrapping the country in as many tentacles, along which they sped as they avoided where possible convolutions, underpasses, and loop-overs, but less successfully the circumlocutions when posting to their fans – the hells angel outriders on their Harleys, clearing the traffic ahead of the speeding motorcade of limos, which one chat-host called:

'This righteous cavalcade of privileged billionaire brats of the new perp industry in their e-chariots, on a mission to replace manifest reality with fake dreams, turn you and me into avatars, rob our kids of a future, poison us with interactive porn, and steal the world from under our feet.'

With the widely publicized invent-slams, which soon went viral, viewers debated maths versus common sense, questioned shopping and argued whether the earth was a shrink-wrapped pizza hologram or a Monsters of the Panty-Verse computer game. The new Corporation scraped up the raw talent universities across the land had cast aside and wrapped them up in FakeReal Associate deals they could never get out from, until they were fired.

Turned out, the Imp-drive was everything the Inventor claimed. However, it was canned shortly before going into production, after the Pentagon deemed that the new Imp-Tech was too disruptive, except for them, which didn't come as a surprise to Fatberg. Anticipating just such a turn, he had already snaffled the only prototypes, M-1, M-2, and M-3.

Too bad the inventor couldn't handle his generous compensation package from the government agency who took over the defense contract under clause 402 of the Strategic Industries Requisition Provisions: Emergency Powers Act, Sub-section C. He was last heard of in a small town on Highway 41, down in the former Everglades. The investigator assigned to his case, reported the subject was in the business of farming 'gators and wasn't doing well, with the drought, no mud for wallowing his dehydrated 'gators, and his increasing consumption of methamphetamine; he was acting out the sad decline of a near genius. Still couldn't remember the man's name. Call him Inventor FR Associate 201. Most likely dead by now, if not from the drugs then from his pet 'gators, which the investigator said wandered freely about the boat house beached in the dried-up lake down in the Never Glades, as the news shows called them now. Shame, Fatberg might have dropped in on him and compared notes about the counting, but now it was too late.

At long last, Fatberg understood his compulsion was, and had always been, about figuring out what the hell the universe would manifest next. Each moment ended in a cliff-hanger, with a null gap you could fall into, before the next moment.

He was never so scared of them as then, as a small child, standing at the bottom of a long flight of stairs, determined to climb the steps on his own. He'd had to figure out the how and where to place his feet. First, his outside leg, making sure his big toe was all the way in, then made his inside leg push up (which was nearest the wall) and lifted his foot over the gap onto the next step. Determined, the jaw proud, his tiny teeth clamped in grim concentration, careful not make a sound, not looking down at his feet in case he put them off and he fell in a gap. One by one, he mounted the risers, the counting the easy part, because he could already count up to fifty-five in just three breaths. Worst was crossing the gaps which he felt reaching up to grab him through the soles of his feet, petrified each time. Looking up, he saw that the red hand of the big round clock above, at the head of the stairs, was counting his steps as it swept round the dial. His foot stopped, it stopped, he moved a fraction, and it moved, also a fraction, like they were playing a game ...

But then the moment was gone, when he heard his father calling him from the garden, where the sun was shining, the light spilling in through the open front door, his father's long shadow stretching an arm and a pointing black finger to where yellow sunlight lapped the gleaming wooden boards at the bottom of the stairs...

*

THE GREAT OLYMPUS GAMES –
SCENE #3 EPISODE 23

'SILENCE!

'But I ...'

'SILENCE I SAID,' Zeus thundered. 'The prisoner has had ample opportunity to respond to the charges. We have heard enough evidence,'

'This is ridiculous,' Prometheuz yelled, his blood rushing to his head all of a sudden, his earbud buzzing as he veered off-script in his first line of dialogue. 'I haven't heard anything. Just what am I charged with? I only just got here!

'HEY!' he cried, jumping back as a sizzling bolt of white fire struck the stone dock, which though non-fungible, felt real enough when he withdrew his scorched fingertips from the seared line on the cheap prop conforming to the outline of the dock, where he had gripped the 3D printed rail. There was a disparity between fungible and non-fungible furniture, sight and touch, combined with the drag of his cumbersome heavy new muscles, as Zeus in his high chair glowered down at him, the biggest fake of all. He felt he had been suckered against his will into the part, not even being told he was playing a prisoner, the dupe of one and all including billions of livestreaming perps. All he wanted to be locked in his cell, safe behind a steel door, with the double blind world, and all in it, shut out.

'SILENCE!' Zeus raised a lightning rod finger. 'OR I WILL STRIKE YOU DOWN.'

'Almighty Father.' Dionysus stepped out and stood, hands clasped humbly before him, craftily looking up under dipped eyelids at Zeus. The Father was leaning out from his high chair above the steep, worn steps cut in the gigantic, clear crystal boulder, jazzed with veins of gold, which supported the almighty father's great throne.

'If I may be allowed to intercede.'

'SPEAK!'

'What I have to say is not for lesser

gods to hear, oh Almighty Father.'

'VERY WELL THEN,' Zeus rumbled, directing a spark at the steps, which lit up. 'APPROACH.'

Taking the opportunity of the first moment he was not the center of the attention, Prometheuz carefully scanned his surroundings. In the foreground, ranged in concentric half circles facing him, were rows of benches divided by an aisle. On the left side, Poseidon sat impassively, while two demigods of the Prosecution debated across him. Across the aisle, however, the first and second row of the benches reserved for the Defense were empty, which figured, Prometheuz thought.

Further back, both sides of the aisle, benches were filling up with gods and their acolytes. Middle of one group, tall Athena unmistakable under a red-crested golden motorcycle helmet, her famous AK 74 automatic assault rifle, which supposedly was solid platinum and 100% real, gripped in her mighty left hand, and the owl that sees everything perched on her broad right shoulder. At the back, between the benches and the ring of non-fungible pillars, ushers walked about in their birthday suits or body suits, either way ridiculous, beaming as they welcomed more gods and their entourages into the vast Hall of Zeus every few seconds.

Each time was heralded by a brilliant flash – red, gold. Hermes was the only god who arrived alone, while Ares made the biggest entrance. Announced by a dark red flash, he blazed in, dressed like a cowboy, except for the horns that poked out of his big Stetson hat. One hand was raised in salute as he stood astride the hood of a bonnet of a red corvette with whitewall tyres and twin mufflers jetting flames, like he was descending on a flying chariot, as might be expected of the God of War.

The illusion of a crowded concourse held all the way to the pillars. Projected in blacklight between them were the invisible, blacklight field distortion lenses, which the make-up girl had said were multi-directional, which he took to mean two-way and brought everything right up close, no matter where you were standing. And it was true; when his gaze lingered on any of the perps shuffling in the outer darkness beyond, their monstrous faces and the eyes on him enlarged, until the hairy warts became hillocks, and their scars crevasses, giving him the feeling he was a hamster in a cage surrounded by ravenous monsters.

None was more grotesque than Medusa. When he picked her out among the perps and focussed on her, she swelled in size until she filled the space between non-fungible pillars. She had a basket of snakes for a head, which fortunately was turned away, otherwise he might have been turned to stone, or so the legend went in his Grandfather's book of Ancient Greek Myths, he suddenly recalled, taking that to be a hopeful sign the elusive story would pop into his mind.

Of course, he knew the monsters ranging the tiers of the make-believe amphitheater beyond the pillars were only avatars. Some, he realized, could be friends, nursing resentments at his elevation to godhood status, joining in the baying mob livestreaming on the Home Pay-2-Perp Service. He hoped not, for their sakes, whenever they came to their senses, in some far-off future when the smog lifted, the Emergency restrictions ended, and the world was not shut-down. For himself, his mind kept shying away from whatever the fuck was coming round the next corner. Just dealing with what was before him was enough.

Seeking distraction, he looked up at the distant dome, which had been likened to a sieve in the chat boxes. Much significance was given to the fact there were 33 windows piercing it, and to their cunning mandala arrangement. From the non-fungible universe beyond into the dome, through the angular little windows, blacklight poured in arabesque isosceles veils, in full glorious holo-vision that consistently got a max 5 on the EyeCandy rating on the V-Travel Trust Guide, and had been compared to the Igazu Falls in South America as they had appeared before they generated electricity.

So those were the heavens. On the set, groups of conspicuously-muscled male gods and equally voluptuous female gods comingled, in pools of blacklight that shafted down from above. Each god glowed, radiating a signature colour – blue, green, gold, red, purple – and every shade in between. Unmistakable, among their entourages of acolytes, hangers on, demigods, and such. Each face a living sculpture, majestic, every kind of twisted, morose, indifferent and beautiful in the same moment, each god having a different portion of each. Lyre birds chirped on their shoulders, shoals of fish swam in the air about them, marking an absence of sea.

Actually, Prometheuz didn't think hardly any of this, or see the fish, though he later thought he had. Instead, apart from the rating on Trust Guide™, the thought string had been beamed into the medulla oblongata of his brain by his iteration - who had been with him all the way from the muscle clinic and, unseen, was perched on the dock at

Prometheuz's elbow, kicking his heels, watching everything and reading the lines no one else saw, converging on the set from billions on HM -BDY, Pay-2-Perp, and all the other livestreaming channels.

*

THE GREAT OLYMPUS GAMES –
SCENE #4 EPISODE 23

'SILENCE IN COURT,' Zeus thundered, bolts of lightning flashing from the non-fungible dark clouds roiling about his great head.

'SILENCE!' he repeated. His great eyes searched the Gods' faces in the hall below for sarcastic expressions and other signs of dissent as they looked back up at him. 'GOOD!' he rumbled, 'I have been informed by… ah…' He frowned, looked down.

'Dionysus, Almighty Father,' Dionysus grinned lopsidedly, 'Your fifth son.'

'Really?' Zeus raised an eyebrow that resembled a thornbush.

'Mnemosyne will help you recall which one I am. She is near, I can summon her, Almighty Father.'

'I need no assistance from the daughter of the Muse to recall your miserable hide, Dionysus, nor the way you took to the wine cup even before you were weaned. Bah! You were a drunkard when a godling, and now you stand before me, in your red cloak of a public defender, still a drunkard, representing another reprobate.' Zeus nodded towards Jake in the dock, before adding in a foghorn boom, for the benefit of anyone in the court not paying attention, 'THE PRISONER.'

'Who, I must point out, has lately been deserted by Mnemosyne and so remembers nothing of the proceedings thus far,' Dionysus interjected, hastily. 'And has not been found guilty for the crimes, Almighty Father.' He offered up his trademark grin. 'Yet!' he added.

'Indeed, I take your point.' Zeus nodded. 'Even though I never heard a more open and shut case.'

'Almighty Father, even you ...' Dionysus pleaded from the steps below.

'Yes I know,' Zeus sighed, heavily. Pointing to a nearby stone column and its inscription, he read out. 'Law Two: no god will be condemned without a fair hearing before his peers. And listen to Law Four. All gods are equal before the Law. I must have been under the influence of Eros when I carved that.' He chortled into his beard. Though restrained, his laughter shook the pillars of the Great Hall, alarming the gods gathered below, who all knew all too well the destruction that often followed Zeus's mirth.

'Almighty Father,' Dionysus pleaded, more forcefully. 'He is the youngest Titan of your generation. Your cousin!'

'Indeed. And long has he troubled me.'

'If not for him, surely for his father and the immortal ichor churning in our veins, Almighty Father,' Dionysus pleaded, hopefully.

'You dare invoke Cronus, my father.' Zeus thundered, still feeling guilty over castrating his father, though not over murdering him.

'I would not dare so to presume.' Dionysus hung his head, looked back at Prometheuz, and winked.

'Hmm,' Zeus rumbled. 'Very well, I will

grant your request, since there is nothing to the contrary to suggest that the, um ...'

'The accused,' Dionysus prompted.

The mighty brow of Zeus furrowed as if Circe had just harrowed it with her plough. Leaning over the arm of his throne, he glared down at Dionysus, who rapidly shrank under the power of his gaze till he was no bigger than a pea, but then rebounded to his usual size.

After a meaningful pause intended to communicate to Dionysus the narrowness of his escape, Zeus continued, 'In consideration of the claims put forwards by my fifth son, his reprobate defender, that Mnemosyne for reasons known only to her sweet immortal self has lately deserted the prisoner, and taken his memory of the proceedings, I rule that his confessions shall be replayed so that he might benefit from witnessing from his own mouth the full account he gave to all gathered here of his crimes.'

*

CHAPTER 5

DBUKSET Channel WKYTUBE: intercept conversation on FakeNet between Dmbwtz and Scoop-a-Perp. Analysis: 72.4-82.8% poss. C.R. P.–

D. I say it's an authentic apparition.

SP. I'm not so sure, the freeze-holo is not at all clear.

D. Five of the six hex-cams follow it as it drops from the dock and walks towards P. on the benches ...

SP. Who doesn't see it, even though he's looking straight at it.

D. Obviously it's invisible to the actors, even Prom, who's closest most of the time.

SP. Could be a hack attack by a rival corporation, like that one years back, in that otherwise totally forgettable FauxReel show, Bo-Peep.

D. I will never forget that. My kids were livestreaming episode five when those demon avatars broke through the V-thing. Fucking wrecked the living room.

SP. How is that possible?

D. At first, I didn't believe it either. But the damage was so extensive. Like a cyclone had passed through. I found my kids quaking under the sofa, where it had been tossed in a corner with the rest of the busted furniture.

SP. You serious?

D. Absolutely, the kids were totally traumatized.

SP. You could have sued.

D. Oh, I contemplated it, to be sure. I V-cammed everything, and for back-up took photos, then got a neighbor to witness the damage. But in the end I decided against.

SP. Why?

D. Well, what finally put me off was the thought of my kids having to relive the trauma every time the case came to court.

SP. Every time?

D. Just supposing we won the first time, with all those lawyers FuxReel keep on the books, it was bound to be appealed to a higher court, and so on, right to the top.

SP. The Supreme Court?

D. Sure, if we got that far.

SP. Might be interesting. Think about it, by the time you got there, you'd be a fully qualified lawyer.

D. You know, I think that's 'bout the most intelligent thing I have ever heard you say.

SP. Why thank you.

D. Seriously, I mean it. But what put me off in the end was imagining my boys being cross-examined under auto-stim, by some dick-brain prof, who can pull out of my boys' minds just anything they want.

SP. They can do that?

D. Uh-huh. I read up on some cases in the court records. One guy who sued FauxReel for messing up his kids' heads ended up convicted of molesting them. Next his wife divorced him, and now he's down in the subs. Happens all the time.

SP. Yea, up one rung, then woops, down a slippery v-snake.

D. I didn't mean it literally.

SP. Hey, you're supposed to be the dumb one.

D. Yes, but switching roles is fun, as you know because you done it before.

SP. Done what? You messing with my head again?

D. Was not aware you had one.

SP. Doh!

*

Turning away as Julius continued jabbering at her, Carrie noticed that the obelisk, which had been to her right a moment before, was now to the left of the little bubble car.

Seen though the dripping perspex bubble, it resembled a giant upright needle, balanced in the smog, seeming to draw etheric phantoms from all around. The eye, where she supposed the base of the column to be, was threaded by a long, spooling line that was tied to the bobbin of the bubble car in which she was trapped with Julius. He was supposed to know where he was going since he was the CEO of the biggest corporation on the planet, with a T/O greater than the combined member nations of the EU, but obviously he was lost for directions.

She didn't have a clue either. The one and only living claimant to the throne of Russia. Herself, she thought, Ms Caroline Emilia Anastasia Romanov aka Erheart, lately of apartment 223 in the Pierspoint Building.

Zip …? She couldn't now remember. Because none of that existed now, only the smog which had stolen the world, and Jake, from her. She wondered if he was better off down in the subs, away from her nagging, which he was always complaining of …

'Why the long sigh?' Julius suddenly said, breaking into her thoughts.

Carrie turned away from her window, then started with fright as a pack bot, in green and gold livery, its pannier piled with packages, loomed in the windshield.

'Watch out!' she yelped, as the bubble car somehow missed it. 'You might have hit the poor thing.'

'Not a chance,' Julius laughed, 'they've got AVT.'

'What's that?'

'Avoidance V-tech, you couldn't run one over if you tried. He's a clever bastard.'

'Who?'

'My closest competitor. Montague-Evans.'

When she gave him a blank look, he added, sneeringly, 'The Bot King, so-called. Ugly things aren't they?'

'They're everywhere, and more so since the universal shut-in.' Carrie said, as she peered into the smog to see where it went, noticing that the obelisk had disappeared and had been replaced by the faint outline of the dome.

'Aren't you going to ask me who's expecting us?'

'The Pope, who else?'

'How'd you guess?'

'Well, you being who you are, us on our way to get married, and that being the Vatican.' She pointed at the dome, which had added colonnades to the left and right sides, and a whole lot of statues besides, since she last looked. 'If my new fantasy life with you was a story in a book, most readers would have already worked that out.'

'Remarkable,' Julius muttered with a little shake of his head as he peered into the smog.

'Tell me, how much did it cost?'

'I'm not sure I quite understand.' Julius frowned.

'Donate, as in build a new cathedral, fund cancer research, send missionaries to the moon,' she laughed. 'What do I know?'

'Oh, I see what you mean,' he said, flashing a disingenuous smile. 'I always leave that to others who are more expert in such matters.'

'So modest!' She grinned.

'Look.' He pointed ahead, over the steering wheel. 'I do believe that is our escort party. Do you see there, coming down those steps?'

'Yes. Not so sure about the face masks, though.' She smiled again at the incongruity, with their steel helmets, breastplates, scarlet hosiery, and the antiquated pointed halberds held by the Swiss Guards, marching two abreast down the steps, as the bubble car drew to a stop below.

Watching the scene from his perch on top of the obelisk, Jake2 smiled to himself.

Now the long spooling line was following the pair up the steps, and through a door into the great Basilica beyond. It was a very obedient line.

*

THE GREAT OLYMPUS GAMES – EPISODE 23 SCENE#5

Prometheuz prised apart an encrusted eyelid with a grimy fingernail, just enough for a splinter of light to irradiate his brain and induce a humungous headache. Bad mistake.

His next mistake was attempting to stand up. The fact he couldn't have done it without the support of a tree did not take away from his sense of achievement as he urinated against it, fortunately without splashing his bare legs too much. At last he risked opening one eye wide enough to make out blurred foliage, stunted trees, and knotty faces leering back at him from gnarled, convoluted boughs and dipping branches. Oh fuck, the party.

Now he remembered Dionysus prancing ahead on his cloven hooves, leading him into a woodland glade towards a ring of drunken satyrs, and gyrating nymphs dancing around a blazing fire, sparks spiraling towards a billion twinkling stars in the clear night sky.

But where the hell was he? More to the point who was he? Oh yea, he remembered, a grossly muscled god with a god-sized hangover. He laughed, and immediately regretted it, feeling at any second his head might disengage from his spine and roll off his shoulders. The tree helped as he slid on his back down its trunk and slumped onto something hard, which lodged in the cleft of his naked buttocks. It was an acorn, he discovered, as once again he settled back onto the damp patch between gnarled tree roots.

So, the stunted trees were ancient oaks – unless of course the trees were non-fungible, he considered as he flicked the acorn away. However, the trunk at his back seemed solid enough.

Uh, it was starting to coming back to him. Dionysus pleading his case in Court, Zeus up in his high chair, Poseidon glaring from the benches of the gods of the Prosecution, perps cruising in the darkness beyond the ring of pillars. Then, after Zeus adjourned the proceedings, and as Prometheuz had been following Dionysus out of the court, he noticed him retrieving the blob from the back of the bench where he'd stuck it. Next thing, the pillars of the great hall had disappeared, and the god was leading him into a clearing in a wood, passing him a bulging wine skin filled with cheap plonk, urging him to drink up and promising him a night such as he would never forget in the long days and nights to come of the next ten thousand years.

He'd balked at that, taking the statement to indicate the god expected a guilty verdict when they returned to court. But instead of denying it, Dionysus produced the blob from his shirt pocket, and before he could stop him promptly pressed it to his ear.

Immediately, over the sounds of revelry from around the fire, he heard Poseidon's unmistakable baritone.

'The delay will not change anything. Zeus will see through all Dionysus' tricks. Prometheuz has had this coming a long time. But I'll only be satisfied when I hear Zeus deliver the maximum sentence.

'Don't worry, Bro,' Dionysus said, reaching out and picking the blob from Prometheuz's ear. 'Poseidon's always absurdly confident until things go against him, which they always do in the end, as when he lost the contest for the sky, which Zeus won of course.' Dionysus looked down at the blob in his open hand. 'There will be a lot more audio on this, some of which will give us the edge when we return to court.' He grinned lopsidedly, then slapped Prometheuz on the back, heartily. 'Drink up, Bro, but don't get too incapable.' He winked, meaningfully.

How could he forget Aphrodite descending into the clearing in a shower of gold dust. Completely naked, of course, since being the most beautiful god of all she had nothing to hide and she never wore a scrap of clothes.

Despite heeding Dionysus' caution, Prometheuz had ended up beating his detumenising dick against the trunk of a gnarled oak, which turned out to be a cheap prop like just about everything else in this dumb reality he'd somehow stumbled into. Drunk, he'd completely forgotten the oak grove was a v-set and billions were livestreaming his performance.

It started off well enough when they grappled, as gods generally do when engaging in foreplay, but then, as he mounted Aphrodite's golden clam and saddled up, hearing loud hooting, he'd glanced round and saw a ring of the perps peeping into the grove, their ogling eyes gleaming in the darkness beyond. Result, instant shriveled dick. But goaded by her golden whip, he renewed his assault, but from a new angle, enduring more lashes and a lot of scorn before he breached and, as they say on Mount Olympus, *god down on her*. His head squeezed between her immortal thighs, he knew despair, but bravely kept grinding on with the stubble on his genoplast-enhanced chin, and the other tools available to him, until she came like a semi-automatic – and he was almost decapitated by her scissor legs.

Then, after she left without a backwards look, in a great huff of golden sparks, Prometheuz stomped about the grove looking around every tree for his trousers. Had the perps run off with them, he wondered, by that time having completely forgotten he was only an actor in a v-production.

*

'Here he comes.' Julius nudged Carrie, as they waited in the Sacristy, where the Swiss Guards had left them in the charge of a tall, taciturn, heavily built priest, who Julius guessed was papal security.

'Oh god,' Carrie muttered to herself, wishing she was wearing a less outlandish outfit than her mix-and match ensemble, she'd picked out from her clothes closet.

Appropriately, as will be explained, the Pope's imminence was announced by the sound of rapidly approaching footsteps.

Unusually, since he was still very much alive, 82-year-old Gregorius XVIII was already considered by Church historians to be one of the greatest reforming popes. However, despite his achievement in reuniting the mother church with the Orthodox Greek and Russian churches which had broken away in

1054, in the 'Great Schism', he was popularly known as the *Walking Pope*.

'My dears,' said the energetic old man in his simple white robes, with his twinkling blue eyes. He held out both hands as he walked towards them, the heels of his famous red shoes clicking on the marble floor.

Behind him came his secretary, a thin, sallow-faced wiry man with beady black eyes behind gold-framed round spectacles, wearing a conservative black suit, patent leather lace-up shoes, and carrying a clipboard in one hand and a gold fountain pen in his other. Behind him, struggling to keep up, came two fat, perspiring priests in black cassocks, who clearly were not used to exercise.

'Ho un matrimonio da officiare. Vai ora, dì alle guardie di essere nella cappella, quando arriviamo lì.' the Pontiff said, with a nod at the two fat priests, who were both obviously relieved to be dismissed, and scuttled away.

'My dear Ms Erheart.' He beamed beatifically as she curtseyed – something she had never done before, but felt impelled to do. 'Or perhaps I should say, Ms Romanov.' He raised an eyebrow, their eyes meeting as she stood up.

'How?' she blurted, totally astonished that he knew her real name.

'My dear,' he said, lightly taking Carrie's hand in his fingers, 'a source of great sorrow to my predecessors, and of course my fellow Patriarchs in our united church, is the terrible tragedy suffered by your family. You have always been in our prayers.'

Half-turning, he extended his other hand. 'Welcome, my dear Julius,' he said. 'Without your great generosity, and the Holy Channels our good friends in FauxReel have provided during this awful Emergency, in one hundred and forty-seven languages no less, the sufferings of the United Church would have been immeasurably greater!'

'It has been our privilege, and a personal honor, Holy Father,' Julius mumbled, uncharacteristically, his head bowed.

'This is such a happy day!' the Pope exclaimed. 'Come, let us walk together. Isn't it wonderful we have the whole of the Vatican to ourselves.'

Walking between them, hand in hand, he led them down a long barrel-vaulted corridor, with Ancient Roman statues at intervals in niches along the walls.

Behind them, scribbling down everything the Pope said, trotted the secretary, who in turn was followed by the taciturn priest.

'I have a confession to make,' the Pope said, in a different tone. 'Since the Emergency began, I have found myself, shall we say, appreciating certain, um, aspects of the restrictions we are all under.'

'Really, Holy Father?' Carrie, who was enjoying her first real exercise (apart from on her treadmill) in three long years, asked.

'Yes, my dear,' he said, 'I am afraid it is true. You are aware what many people call me?'

'*The Walking Pope?*'

'Yes my dear,' he nodded pontifically, slowing his pace slightly for the benefit of Julius, who though fit, and never shut-in like 99% of the population these past 3 years, had started panting. 'And until recently, never was a name less deserved.'

'How is that, Holy Father?' Carrie asked, politely.

'Well, my dear, ever since I entered the Church, I have always been the *walking* something or other. First I was called the Walking Novice, and later the Walking *Priest*. Life was simple then, there were no limousine drivers to become unemployed if I didn't permit them to take me everywhere. With every elevation the walking became more difficult, as more obstacles were placed in my way. As a Bishop in Africa I had to exercise my ecclesiastical powers just to be permitted to walk the last few miles to any village or town I visited in the course of my duties, and even then I had to walk at the pace of the slowest of my entourage.

'My ambulatory difficulties were only compounded when I was appointed a cardinal, and of course by then the entourage had considerably swelled in size. I didn't think things could possibly get any worse, until, for my sins, my fellow cardinals plotted to make me pontiff, and unfortunately, after several recounts, succeeded!' He laughed. 'My favourite TV serial on the very limited choices we had then on Vatican Cable became *The Prisoner*, perhaps because, cut off as I found myself in the papal apartments, I soon identified with the protagonist. But then that was a decade ago, before this, um...'

The Pope lowered his voice, so his secretary, taking notes a discrete five paces behind, could not hear. 'The *blessed* Emergency came along,' he laughed, 'and I discovered that to my great joy I could make a complete circuit of these buildings, which according to the pedometer on my leg is twenty-two point two two kilometers, and without ever once stepping outside.'

They had reached the end of the long corridor of statues. 'Now,' the Pope smiled, 'I must stop talking as before us, we have one of the great wonders of Christendom, which also I believe has been inspirational for our friends at FauxReel with their new popular V-show.'

'Please don't repeat that to others, Holy Father,' Julius interjected.

'Why, my son?' the Pope, asked, stopping in the entrance of the Sistine Chapel.

'My critics would use it against me, Holy Father, and, um, I don't think it would go down too well with our core audience if they learned we modelled Zeus on the image Michelangelo painted of Almighty God.' Julius pointed up at the ceiling. 'And all the other elements we borrowed, with your permission, of course, Holy Father,' he added, hastily.

'Well, that was entertainment for the masses then, I suppose,' the Pontiff sighed. 'It was a very different world when Michelangelo painted his murals.'

Both Julius and Carrie had only wanted a simple wedding. So they got a simple pastor to bless them – the Pope! Well, Julius was who he was. Besides, he was owed a favor or two for the lifeline FauxReel had extended to the Mother Church since the start of Emergency.

The place was the Sistine Chapel under the famous mural of the story of Genesis. On the wall before them loomed Michelangelo's other great mural, The Last Judgement. One giant figure in particular kept drawing Carrie's attention. Crouched with one hand over an eye, he had an expression of utmost horror on his face, as two devils dragged him by the legs down to the fires of hell. Something about him reminded her of Jake, not so much his physique, though there were similarities, nor his anguished expression, but most definitely his uncovered eye – which she felt watched her intently throughout.

The ceremony was just as they wanted – short and simple. All that was required from the Pope were the words, 'Ti pronuncio uomo e moglie,' which his secretary wrote on a lined page on his clipboard. The Pope added his initials below, then one of the Swiss Guards standing by was summoned to sign his name, and it was done – they were married!

Bi-located in the giant's eye on the wall mural, Jake2 was curious about the movements of the v-cams, all of which had been tracking the happy couple ever since they entered the chapel.

The marriage ceremony was of no interest him, other than that it was the direct result of his manipulations and as such entirely satisfactory. From the lines which enmesh the world, that intersected the space, he should have been able to determine who or what was viewing the happy couple, but after he identified the one line out of all those intersecting the space, whenever he attempted to trace the line back to its source, a dangerous elemental which he perceived as a giant snake blocked him – a snake that looked suspiciously like the one tempting Eve, in the ceiling panel …

*

Feeling his head could explode at any moment, Prometheuz closed his eyes. But he couldn't shut out the images of himself which Mnemosyne, who was supposed to be his sister, projected in the air before him.

Himself, if he was to believe his eyes, shaping the evil manikins from clay, then breathing life into them.

'That alone merited banishment from Olympus,' Poseidon thundered, levelling his trident accusingly at him.

But worse, the clay was mixed with dirt, which the imposter had secretly collected from the Proving Grounds where the Gods settled disputes, upon which, over the ages, had been spilt much immortal ichor – blood, he was supposed to understand.

Again, he had been unable to deny the evidence presented before him in holographic detail.

That immortal blood, and his breath, had bestowed on the perps consciousness, an attribute which was the property of the gods alone. But the worst crime had been to steal fire from Zeus's hearth and give it to the perps, along with the secrets of writing, numbers, and artifice. Now fires raged across Gaia, the playground planet that Zeus had constructed for the pleasure of the Gods and its resident spirits – all the different kinds of nymphs, nereids, satyrs, dryads, panes and tritons that looked after its precious mountains, pastures, forests, wetlands, pools lakes, springs, streams, rivers, seas and oceans, and the habitats of its many species of creatures. But not satisfied wreaking destruction across what had been the loveliest of planets in all of Creation, now the perps were plotting to storm heaven and overthrow Olympus.

'Do you still deny your crimes, perp lover!' Poseidon demanded, brandishing his trident.

'Yes, absolutely!' Prometheuz stubbornly insisted. 'All the evidence has been faked. None of this is down to me. Heaven knows I hate the perps as much as the next god! Ever since I was a little Titan I ...'

'I have heard enough!' Zeus thundered, cutting off Prometheuz mid-peroration. 'Despite all his denials, the Prisoner is clearly guilty, of all the charges.'

He glared down at Prometheuz. 'Have you anything to say in mitigation before I pronounce sentence?'

'This is a set up!' Prometheuz protested. 'I've been framed.'

'Silence, prisoner.' Zeus raised a hand threateningly.

'Oh go and fuck yourself, Almighty Father. I've had enough of this shit.'

As the perspicacious reader may already have noted, Jake had become so absorbed in his role he had begun to believe he really was Prometheuz.

This is a danger of the technique of method acting, particularly for amateur thespians who can fail to recognize when they have reached the point of no return, beyond which there is no way back to who they were when they started playing the part.

*

CHAPTER 6

Conversation on the FauxReel Culture Vultures Channel: 235:hrs. 13/10/43.

'We've had all this before!'

'Not so, Petronella. If you think back, they have reprised it with some very significant differences.'

'You mean *slightly* different, which you know well, Elliot, amounts to much the same. Really, it's an outrage!'

'Perhaps you're exaggerating a little, Petronella.'

'The cheek! I could peck the eyes out of the chicken brain genius who dreamed-up this cheap wheeze, really I could. How much do the poo pellet counters upstairs fucking save? I'm so disappointed, Elliot. And to cap it off, I discover that this goddamn vulture avatar can't cry. If you could see me now in my v-tent, Elliot.'

'Hush, Petronella, we don't talk of that, remember. Look on the bright side, I think it's a plot curve.'

'What do you mean? Preposterous! Plots need to keep to the point, not stray and go curvy. Really!

'Think of it, Petronella, this might be the most vital twist, when the trajectory goes bendy. A T-bendy they call it. *(looks down)* I think. Not sure about the 'y' though.'

'And tonight you, Elliot, bandy bendy words about rather more than usual!'

'If you'd listen, instead of squawking so loudly, you might hear ...'

'What?

'Well ...' *(pause)*

'You were going to say *(yawn)* to expect a great scene.'

'No ... I mean, uh, yes, *absolutely*, Petronella! The more disappointment you feel now, the greater will be your surprise when ...'

'When what, Elliot? What am I to expect?' *(fluffs breast feathers)*

'Gore, Petronella, gore. I predict there will be so much gore, as never before. Enough even to satisfy you *(laughs)*, my dear. Or perhaps I will turn everyone to stone, trigger a monster quake on Mount Olympus and bring down the non-fungible pillars of Zeus' temple with a full-on stare of my three hundred and thirty-three pairs of snake eyes *(Shakes head – Medusa snakes wiggle)*. What do you think!? *(superior smile)*

'My tally app counts six hundred and sixty-six snake eyes *(peers at each pair in turn)*. Which ones are yours, Elliot?'

'You are entering dangerous territory *(note of venom)*. Take care, Petronella.'

'What? You worried that I might guess?' *(sinister titter)*

'We all have our secrets, Petronella. I always respect yours.'

'Oh ho! I didn't see much evidence of that when you crossed the set and were an item with Gerald in the Basilisk Pen.'

'Now, you know we don't give other's names. Remember, rules of the game. The privacy of the perp is always paramount. That's basic, Petronella. Basic! And never you forget it.' *(snake hisses)*

'How I wish I could *(pronounced squawk)*, every time you remind me.'

*

Dazed after the rushed preparations for the next scene, in which he was alternatively pummeled, told to sit up, lie down, had his head put in restraints, was turned over, scrubbed, force-fed liquids by tube and enemas, his mind was as empty of thought as the chassis of a car shunting along a factory assembly line. Only in his case it wasn't robots installing parts, but cosmeticians, masseurs, chiropractors, dental technicians, and other specialists working him over. All the while his voice coach walking alongside, making him repeat the lines she recited again and again.

As has already been noted, confused as to who he was at the start of the process, by the time they were through with him in the body shop located below the set, his old self was as distant to him as the young child is to the adult. To be sure, in a corner of his mind, the old Jake was still there, but out of reach of is manufactured new self. This 'immortal' creature of enhanced genoplast ever-renewing flesh, this sacrificial victim with such exaggerated musculature was finally ready for all those monstrous perps cruising in the darkness, beyond the set.

'Cooeee!

Fatberg groaned, as he recognized the familiar voice. 'Speak of the devil,' he said in a resigned tone, regretting having accepted the call from the CEO of Styx2U on his private v-number.

'First sign of madness!

'What do you mean?' Fatberg scowled back at the cocky homunculus in a green suit with its gold lapels. He was standing hands on hips on the little pedestal, where he had just manifested next to Fatberg's elbow.

'Well, I don't see anyone else in the cabin with you,' the little man said, archly, pointedly looking about.

'Oh I see,' Fatberg sniffed. 'Your name came up earlier in conversation, that's all. What do you want, Montague? I'm busy right now.'

'Actually, I called to congratulate you!'

'About what?' Fatberg's eyes narrowed.

'Oh I see,' Fatberg sniffed. 'Your name came up earlier in conversation, that's all. What do you want, Montague? I'm busy right now.'

'Actually, I called to congratulate you!'

'About what?' Fatberg's eyes narrowed.

'On getting married, dear chap. Had I known earlier I would have sent you a big bunch of something smelly. It's about time! Ha. And your mystery new wife did look lovely in that extraordinary –'

'How did you find out?' Fatberg snapped.

'On FauxReel, where else? It's all over the v-waves.'

'I wonder, who was the source?' Fatberg said pointedly.

'Not me, old boy, you have to look elsewhere for that. Lots of speculation about your lovely new wife by the way. You would have thought nothing else had happened in the world today. I must say, dear chap, it really was a coup getting the Pope to do the honors.'

'Goodbye, Montague!' Fatberg said, firmly, peremptorily ending the v-call just as Carrie, her hair still damp after taking a shower, entered the little cabin. She was wearing a Japanese kimono she'd discovered among the designer outfits in her voluminous clothes closet.

'Who was that?' she asked, settling into the other chair.

'Nobody!' he said. Then, when she raised an enquiring eyebrow, he added with a calculated shrug, 'You know, business.'

'Poor Julius.' She patted his arm, 'No escape even on our honeymoon.'

'Did you have a nice nap?'

'Hmm, yes. I feel so refreshed,' she smiled, 'and all the better because in the rush to leave the apartment I forgot my handheld.'

'You did?' Fatberg could barely disguise his relief.

She nodded. 'Where are we flying over now?'

'Ah let me see.' Julius peered at his instrument panel. 'Yes, as of now DD four two, point four-nine nine-nine eight.'

'Julius, you should know by now, all those figures mean nothing to me. I need a name.'

'Ok.' Julius typed the numbers on a pad. 'Ah, apparently we are directly over the highest point in the Caucasus Mountain range, which is eighteen thousand six hundred and –'

'Julius!' Carrie snapped, 'What did I just say?'

*

CHAPTER 7

THE GREATEST OLYMPUS GAMES –
EPISODE 23 SCENE#6

(Banner Headline Emblazoned Across the Sky)

'DAY 1 – THE NEXT 100,000 YEARS'

From afar, it was a gash on the face of a blasted mountain-top.

Closer to, however, the gash was revealed to be the gaping mouth of a cave which, though entirely natural and shaped by the elements alone, had perfectly formed granite lips drawn back in an evil grimace, and a great lolling tongue of purple stone projecting between the bared teeth, on which the giant lay sleeping with his legs and arms spread, his bound wrists and ankles shackled to a massive porphyry slab by golden manacles. Yea, you guessed it …

Prometheuz opened his eyes and groaned. Where was he? Oh yes, Mount Caucasus, where the smith of the gods, Hesiod, and his dwarves had brought him in the dead of the night, before the lame fucker, who was Prometheuz's nephew, limped back to Olympus, leaving him shackled to cold stone to start his sentence.

And as if one hundred thousand years wasn't enough, Zeus had added another punishment – but what? It was at the back of his mind, a story, or something he had been told a long, long time ago. If only Mnemosyne had been near, he could have asked her help to recover the memory. But now there was no one around save for annoying sprites of the wind ruffling his hair as dawn broke and the sun rose over a distant range of mountains.

No god is as cruel as Zeus. It was only when his Zeus smiled down on him when pronouncing judgement that at last he realized how true the ancient Olympian saying was. *No god is as cruel as Zeus.* As one, the assembled gods gasped. Mnemosyne's eyes had widened in horror, while his attorney, Dionysus, hung his head for shame. Even Poseidon, over in the Prosecution benches, was visibly shocked. All the gods assembled in Zeus's great hall knew that the sentence was a warning to each and every one of them, but only Prometheuz got to pay the price.

And now, spread-eagled (now there's a word) to a slab stone, sheltered from the worst of the elements in the mouth of a cave, Prometheuz could only follow the progress of Helios's fiery chariot, as in his god-addled mind he now thought of the sun. One moment it was dawning over the range of mountains to the east, and the next, it seemed, it was careering towards its zenith.

Looking down from the summit of the mountain where he was bi-located on the set, Jake2 didn't feel the slightest sympathy for his material double chained to a flat rock below.

What Jake had coming was payback, and entirely proportionate, in his view. He wanted him to suffer as he had, trapped in a shadow existence all these years, his only escapes when Jake slept and he took over. But even then, still he wasn't free of him – whatever Jake had been obsessing on earlier that day chasing him down the REM dreamways – the effects of alcohol being the worst come Friday nights, after Jake got drunk with his pals. Then his perceptions became clouded, and his confused state left him vulnerable to attack by the elementals which roamed the lower reaches of the dream world – iterations of the same perps now prowling the set amongst them.

All in all it had been a nightmare existence, playing second fiddle to Mr Nice Guy Jake, as he was widely perceived in the material world, but whom Jake2 knew as his cruel jailer until the day he'd been expressed from bondage by means of an AI program. Free at last, the tables were turned, he was a shadow player no longer and was in charge of the script of their twinned lives.

Half blinded by the sun, which was now dipping towards the western horizon, Prometheuz squinted up at the orange flecked sky, wondering if the speck he had just seen high above was a bird or a dust mote in his eye?

He hoped it was dust, because somehow he felt that a bird was associated with whatever he had been trying to remember, and he knew it was not a pleasant memory. For sure it was a bird up there, he realized, after trying to blink it away, but bigger. Now he could make out its great wings, as it circled closer. Was it a vulture, perhaps? No, definitely an eagle. Vultures had scrawny necks and red wattles, whereas there was nothing scrawny about this raptor, or the intent in the black eyes, as it looked down on him, the sharp point of its razor beak gleaming red from the setting sun as it swept down on him, claws extended.

'Aaaaaaaah!' he screamed, impotently, rattling his chains as the great eagle landed on his chest in a flurry of feathers, its cruel claws raking his exposed flesh, the huge wings *blotting out the setting sun,* wrapping him in shadow deeper than the blackest night.

Let there be blood. Buckets of it. Wasn't that what the perps wanted most of all? Yea, and the non-fungible entrails and real gobbets of genoplast flesh that splattered their monstrous, upturned faces as the scene ended and Zeus's eagle soared off into a non-fungible sunset.

How the perps loved it, but yet the scene was an anti-climax, as so often when what has been keenly anticipated comes around at last.

Not so for Jake2 watching from the summit of the mountain, for whom revenge was sweet, knowing that this scene with the eagle tearing at his material double's innards would be played out, over and over for the next hundred thousand years, as Zeus had ruled when he pronounced sentence on the prisoner.

INTERMISSION

Pity poor Prometheuz as the hex-v-cams pulled away, and under cover of darkness the 3D-printed mountain construction sank below the v-set, where a medic team was on standby with the best specialist equipment – heart monitors, defibrillators, IV drips, transfusion machines and supplies of O-positive blood to replace what he had lost, once they had staunched his bleeding.

'Please don't struggle, Mr Cousins,' the medic holding his head in a vice-like grip said, soothingly.

Working as a team, the other medics sutured the livid wounds on his chest and stomach - which by a miracle of genoplast tech had already begun to heal – attached an IV drip to his right arm, inserted a hose into his rectum and flushed out his colon, before swabbing him down.

'Who in heaven's name is this 'Cousins'?' the patient roared, rattling his chains that bound him to the rock. 'I keep telling you I am –'

'Hush now, lie back, please, you need to rest.'

'Gods help me,' the patient groaned, slumping back against the rock to which he was still chained. 'Give me wine, anything for the pain,' he pleaded.

'Jake ...'

Unlike the other masked faces looking down on him, this one was female, her eyes kindly and concerned.

'Jake, it's me,' the voice coach said, taking off her mask. 'Ah, I can see you recognize me now.' She smiled. 'The medics are almost finished now, and I promise you'll feel better soon.'

'Something for the pain, please,' he pleaded.

'We're not allowed to give you

anything.'

'Why?' he groaned.

'Unfortunately the contract you signed stipulated no drugs, which includes anesthetics. Nothing we can do to change that, I am sorry to say.'

'You're sorry! You're fucking sorry! How do you think I feel?' he raged.

'Jake, you are only hurting yourself,' she insisted.

'Gods, remove these chains!' he yelled, rattling them furiously.

'Sorry, but I can't help you there either, Jake.'

'You can't, really, truly?' He stared piteously up at her, tears streaming from his eyes.

'When the last Prom walked out on the set it cost FauxReel billions. *Billions,*' she repeated, emphatically. 'So I am afraid you are just going to have to get used to your golden restraints, which after all, are fur-lined. But, look on the bright side, Jake, with your marvelous new self-repairing genoplast flesh, in just a few hours you'll be ready to face anything.'

'Yea, Prom,' the medic looking on from over her shoulder tittered. 'Ready for Zeus' big bad eagle, heh heh ...'

Pleased to have successfully consummated his marriage, Julian had left Carrie sleeping in her bed, downstairs in her suite of rooms.

His performance (as he thought) was altogether up to the standards he'd maintained over previous years with a succession of Pricilla sex dolls, which he always disposed of after the act (dropped into the smog from a great height being his preferred method) because then they were shop-soiled – by him. His feelings towards Carrie, he freely admitted, if only to himself, were complex. Though not a virgin, and therefore in that sense used goods, he was prepared to overlook her second-hand status in the marriage stakes, on account of the satisfaction he took from the tortures being inflicted on her ex-partner, whose progress on The Greatest Olympus Games show he was avidly following on his hand-held as he lounged in his silk dressing gown, alone (as he thought) in his cabin.

'What are you laughing at?' Carrie said, suddenly appearing at his side.

'Oh, nothing.'

'Can I see it?' she said, holding out a hand.

'Woops, it's gone.' He smiled, nervously. 'Clicked the wrong button! You'd-a thought I knew how to work them better by now. Sorry.'

'So, after we make love for the very first time, you watch porn. Is that what I now have to expect, Julius?'

'Not at all!' he waxed indignant, sitting up in his chair. 'I would never do that.'

'So what was it?'

'Well,' he sighed. 'Ok yes, in one sense, maybe it was porn, even though it was business.'

'Make up your mind, Julius,' she glowered.

'I was just vetting auditions for a new comedy live sex show we have planned for the end of the year. Sorry if I seemed to be enjoying it, but it is work, because I have to give the final say so on which actor gets picked for what role.'

*

CHAPTER 8

V-RIZON – *Serving the V-industry, since V-Genesis.*

On Saturday, 11/7/37 The global livestreaming audience of Episode 5 of FakeReel's latest adult-only blockbuster, The Greatest Olympus Games, peaked at a staggering 5.5 billion, which is 0.2 billion more than the previous record for a livestreamed show.

V-Rizon is an equal opportunities employer. Company motto: *Pursuing excellence beyond and below the horizon.* Annual t/o $(US) 64.277 trillion. V-Rizon is a division of STYX2U Corp. Inc., Registered Office, Box 346, The Hub, New Nautilus City, the Pacific Shelf. Latitude: 39.484589 Longitude: 124.90984

_____

With a sigh, Montague-Evans looked up from the illumined holo display over on his desk, where the little icon of a radioactive turd showed the progress of the Pizza Hut.

It was presently over Pakistan, heading to its next destination.

A bottle-nosed dolphin-bot, trailing an empty pannier and returning to base for more packages, glided past the thick window glass of his office in New Nautilus, 600 fathoms below the surface of the Pacific Ocean, some 220 miles off the coast of California.

The future, Montague firmly believed, lay below the smog, not above it. Out in international waters, Governments had no jurisdiction, there were no dumb planning restrictions to get around, or petty officialdom, with their hands out for bribes. Even better, two hundred miles from the coast, no one owned the seabed, when the equivalent was not true of high altitudes, where Fatberg was building his condos for the super-rich.

Though his preparations for the next stage of his master plan to bring down FakeReal had been meticulous in every respect, Montague couldn't help worrying something might still go wrong before the outsourced covert operation started later that day.

Fatberg was such a lucky bastard. Dirt never seemed to stick to the teflon dick. He'd lost count of how many times his arch rival had over-reached himself and apparently been heading for disaster, only to come up smelling of petunias and even richer than before after his latest megalomaniac project went belly-up, losing his investors' fortunes but never a dollar of his.

Like his ridiculous 10,000 Towers to Save the World, which turned out to have increased atmospheric CO_2 rather than reversing it as had been promised. But against all the facts, such was FauxReel's control of the v-waves, what should have gone down in history as Fatberg's Folly was widely perceived to have been a noble failure, leading

Montague to speculate his hated rival had the magic algorithm of popularity up his sleeve. The news of his recent marriage, which had already gone viral on the v-waves, would do the same, unless it could be made to seem ridiculous in the eyes of the world. Hence what he had planned for FauxReel's flagship v-show in exactly 22 minutes – an intervention calculated to coincide with peak streaming figures. All totally deniable, of course …

THE GREAT OLYMPUS GAMES –

EPISODE 24 SCENE #1

(Banner Headline Emblazoned Across The Sky)

– DAY 2: Prometheuz's Sentence –

'Only 99,999 YEARS, 364 DAYS, *and counting …'*

Groaning, Prometheuz opened his eyes. Mount Caucusus, where else? The golden light of dawn suffusing the sky, announcing day two of his sentence, had arrived. If only he could sleep out the next – what was it – yea, 99,999 YEARS 364 DAYS he had left to serve.

'Fuck you, Zeus!' he screamed, rattling his chains. 'Fuck Poseidon, fucking Hesiod, fuck Aphrodite up every orifice, and clusterfuck Dionysus Piss hole Dionysus, on Mount Olympus or wherever you are. One day, one beautiful day, I swear I will have my revenge on all of you …'

Fucking nothing, not even an echo, from the far mountaintops. He could have taken anything but this blind Olympian indifference to his fate. No god cared one jot for him ...

A faint sensation of warmth seeped into his bones as, in a blaze of glory, the sun god Helios' fiery chariot crested the far ridge of mountains.

Lying on his back, manacled by his wrists and ankles to a bed of cold stone, all Prometheuz could do was scan the sky and wait for Zeus's eagle to descend and once again rip into him with its great beak and cruel claws. Overnight his belly had completely healed, and appeared smooth as a baby's bottom. From his limited perspective, flat on his back, he couldn't see so much as a mark, far less a scar of yesterday's gaping wounds to his chest and stomach – his godlike abs were like new, his self-repairing genoplast flesh totally unblemished – Yea, ripe for ruination once again. How he envied humankind their short lives and merciful death, which granted an end to pain. Not for them protracted tortures, such as he was going to have to endure for … what was it again? Prometheuz groaned once more. Yea, the next 99,999 YEARS 364 DAYS, *and counting.*

Contrary to what he thought, Prometheuz was not alone.

Always his iteration was watching— even as he wove together the storylines of Fatberg, Carrie, and now Montague Evans, into a tapestry of silken threads.

You heard it first on **the FakeBlack**
TRUTHChannel.

'Question everything,
'Deny nothing ...'
(Wilt Whatman)
ID or IT? What comes first?

If you guessed, ID – wrong! No matter where they are born, whatever the culture or in which country, babies always start off as It. Isn't 'It' cuddly. 'It's' so lovely. Oh, can I hold 'it'.' That doesn't last of course. As more and more IDentity traits come to the fore, so the ITeration fades from view. Consequently, by the time the child reaches 5 years old, invariably the ITeration has completely receded into the background – and thereafter only manifests in dreams and altered mind body states.

Dawn had come and gone, noon was well past, and now, as Helios' fiery chariot dipped towards the jagged horizon, at last the moment arrived which the record 5.5 billion livestreaming the Go Games had been waiting for …

But what was this?

As Zeus' mighty eagle swooped down onto poor helpless Prometheuz, chained to his rock, three illuminated figures appeared at his side. Their sudden manifestation elicited a collective gasp from the 5.5 billion audience, the vast majority of whom instantly recognized the familiar face of Fatberg. A smaller though still significant proportion of the audience recognized the second figure to be the Pope, standing in a characteristic pose, one hand raised, clearly blessing the other two figures, facing him, heads bowed. However, only one individual out of that vast audience knew who the third figure was.

'Carrie!' Prometheuz cried, completely forgetting the pain of the eagle's great claws raking his genoplast flesh. His anguish knew no bounds, for he had realized, this was a marriage ceremony he was seeing, and it was the Pope who was pronouncing Fatberg and Carrie man and wife.

Too late, the message which flashed across the v-set, before the livestream footage was abruptly cut-off …

HACK-ATTACK-ALERT- HACK-ATTACK-ALERT …

The moment of high drama which the episode had been building towards was lost. Now all the audience (with one exception) wanted to know was the backstory of the mystery woman who had just married the most eligible bachelor in the entire world.

*

CHAPTER 9

Reuters reports: analysis of data recorded by the 152 stations of the Global Seismographic Network show the collective gasp of the estimated 5.5 billion audience of the GOGames, as they recognized the face of Fatberg, slowed the rotation of the planet by .125 of a second before it resumed its normal speed of rotation, 3.3 minutes later.

The mystery woman was soon identified as Caroline Erheart, after she was named by the former director of an obscure dance company from New Zealand which had disbanded at the start of the Emergency. However, the questions surrounding the former professional dancer only deepened.

Was she, as the host of the Saturday morning batbox show alleged, the ex-partner of the unknown actor drafted in to play Prometheuz in the FauxReel's blockbuster V-show, the GOGames? And if so, what was his connection to Fatberg, who, it was understood, had selected him over the other candidates auditioned for the role. Further investigations revealed that her supposed father, John Erheart, who had died some years before in a mountain climbing accident which was never properly explained, was in fact her guardian, and only took on the role after her Russian émigré parents and her grandmother were all murdered in their Paris apartment by unknown assailants, when she was only three years old.

Like everywhere else, speculation over these and other questions concerning Fatberg's bride was at fever pitch in Kathmandu, which was their next destination. The ancient capital of Nepal was fortunate in being situated above the prevailing smog-belt covering the Indian sub-continent, and so the emergency regulations pertaining in cities at lower altitudes, which forbid public gatherings, did not apply there.

Consequently, when the Pizza Hut landed the next morning in Durbar Square, opposite the royal palace of Hanumandhoka, a large crowd was already gathered in early morning sunshine behind metal barricades, which had been hastily erected by recently re-employed royal guards, resplendent in their new uniforms, to welcome the happy couple.

Prominent among the placards raised above the massed heads of the cheering throng, was a long banner painted with the words: *'All Nepal wishes esteemed Fatberg and his lovely bride a happy honeymoon.'*

'Does that really say what I think it does,' Carrie said, leaning over the rail of the observation deck and pointing to the banner.

'A bit over the top, isn't it,' Fatberg sniggered. 'It seems we are the talk of Kathmandu, sweetie.'

'So who let that cat out of the bag?' she said, accusingly, turning to face him. 'Our marriage was supposed to be secret.'

'I promise you I never … Oh no!' He clapped his forehead, as he suddenly realized this was all to do with the hack attack on the GO Games, which had started exactly eight hours thirty-two minutes before. 'Montague, you bastard!' he glowered.

'What are you saying?' she demanded.

'I know who's behind this. Montague-Evans. The bot king, so-called. How I hate him.'

Of course, when it comes to Fatberg, there are levels and levels. As he had correctly supposed, Montague was behind the hack attack. But though his arch-rival was also responsible for leaking what had already become known as the 'marriage tapes' to the media, in that Montague had only beaten him to the punch by a few days. Fatberg was a master of self-publicity, and despite his assurances to Carrie, he would never have passed on such an opportunity as the v-cam recording of the secret ceremony in the Vatican presented.

However, Fatberg had only planned to leak the material *after* he had concluded (successfully, he assumed), the stalled negotiations with the new Nepalese government, which was his real purpose in coming to Kathmandu, however much Carrie had always wanted to see the sights.

Over the past three years, much had changed in Kathmandu.

The city's smog-free status, which was almost unique among capital cities of the world, had attracted many wealthy new residents, who lived in the shiny high-rise developments which now ringed the old city. The exponentially increasing gap between rich and poor had fueled much resentment amongst the mostly impoverished local population.

In the two weeks since the King had been restored to power, the simmering tensions in the Old City erupted on three successive nights of rioting, which were put down with great brutality by the militarized police working in concert with armed security contractors, employed by the corporate owners of the new developments – foremost among which was the property division of FakeReal.

Clearly something had to be done, otherwise the new wealth flooding into the city would soon go elsewhere, but what, exactly? Only Fatberg had the answer, as ever. But his price for furnishing the solution was high. Very, very high.

*

THE GREAT OLYMPUS GAMES - EPISODE
25

(Banner Headline Emblazoned Across The
Sky)

– DAY 3: Prometheuz's Sentence –

'Only 99,999 YEARS, 363 DAYS *and counting!'*

'Not good, not good,' the CEO of
Styx2U, Montague Evans, mumbled to
himself, oblivious to the leatherback turtle
(which were thought to be extinct), nosing
past the thick glass of his office window some
600 fathoms below the surface of the Pacific
Ocean. He was scanning the threads on the
chat-boxes following the latest GOGames
show, which he had livestreamed in his V-
room only an hour before.

Instead of the audience figures
plummeting after the plug was pulled on the
previous episode, as he had confidently
anticipated, this time they were actually up at
an incredible 5.7 billion, which was a new

world record for any livestreamed show. Worse still, support was now building across all sectors for the dud actor in the main role (drafted in after Montague had bribed the previous one to walk out) over his anguished reaction to the second hack attack, in which the mystery woman had been named as Carrie Erheart and revealed to be his ex-partner.

Once again, against all expectations, Fatberg had benefited, when by now his reputation should have been well into negative territory. Instead, it was up again on Trustpilot, at an unbelievable 7.9, way above any other CEO, and three clear points ahead of his own trust rating. It seemed there was no way to make mud stick to the teflon dick, he considered ruefully, as he clicked onto the next feed.

'What the ..? Montague gasped, staring goggle-eyed at the thread that jumped out at him from the screen of his handheld. 'Of all the lucky bastards … No! No! No!' he protested loudly, to a deity he didn't believe in, 'Please God don't let this be true!'

*

Carrie was out shopping when the news got through to the palace.

His Royal Highness, King Girvanyuddha Bikrama Shah II, was even more impressed after the Russian ambassador's phone call was finally answered. The loud ringing had continued for two minutes 45 seconds according to Fatberg's calculations, until a royal equerry who was in attendance managed to locate the antiquated bakelite telephone, which hadn't rung for several years, under some bejeweled cushions.

'It's for you!' the King said, after answering and exchanging pleasantries with the ambassador, a new note to his Highness' baritone voice suggesting he was feeling a little upstaged as he held out the handset to Fatberg.

'Yes, I am … Yes, you are speaking to me, Mr Ambassador. No, no, she's out presently … What …? No, no. Shopping. You know, women … Ha ha … What did you say..? Yes, the world over … I am sure she … um her Royal Highness will be delighted to accept the invitation. Saint Basil's you say. The President insists. Uh huh. Protocol, yes. I'll instruct my appointments manager to get back to you, to make necessary arrangements once I, ah, have, um, discussed things with her ... Yes, indeed, delighted. The pleasure is mutual ... Please pass on my regards to your esteemed President. Thank you again ... Goodbye.'

Looking back on his audience with the King, Fatberg realized it was the phone call that clinched the deal.

Carrie being who she now was had elevated him in the eyes of the King to her royal consort, the consort of the Tsarina of all Russia in all but name, prior to her coronation in Saint Basil's cathedral in Moscow.

He was the owner of the highest mountain of all, (which the Nepalese called Sagarmatha, meaning "the Head of the Earth touching the Heaven.") and soon to be renamed The Fatberg, on GPS and the next editions of the atlases of the world, once the details of the compensation package with the Nepalese government were finalized. A few ticks and dots were all that was remained to complete after the King and he shook on deal. He was on top of the world. What could go wrong now?

*

It started out as a spontaneous demonstration by a few neighbors, leaning out of the unsealed and open windows of their apartments, chanting 'Free Prom! Free Prom! The chanting quickly spread, until it rang out in streets around the city, and then across the whole world. At last the pent-up rage, engendered by three years of the universal shut-in, had found expression, not just in the support for Prometheuz, who had become emblematic for the plight of the great majority, but the hatred people everywhere had for their corporate captors, who had trashed the world and robbed them of so much. And center stage, head and shoulders above the rest, who else but Fatberg, now firmly in the frame as the chief culprit to blame ...

The story continues, in 3rd book of the XREAL Series, which will be released later in 2022.

INKISTAN
.COM

Will Lorimer is the author of 14 novels, find them on Inkistan.com

Discover Will's Art on willlorimer.com

Printed in Great Britain
by Amazon

18615411R00233